the Antique Chef

Cover artist: Lynda Bell, 'The Guardians'

the
ANTIQUE
Chef

— a novella by —

KAYLEEN M. HAZLEHURST

Revised Edition published 2026
First published in New Zealand in 2023 by
Blue Dragonfly Press

National Library of New Zealand Cataloguing-in-Publication Data
Hazlehurst, Kayleen M, 2023
The Antique Chef / Kayleen M. Hazlehurst

ISBN 978-0-473-66233-2 (International Edition)

Designed and distributed in New Zealand by
The Copy Press, 141 Pascoe Street,
Annesbrook, Nelson, 7011, New Zealand
www.copypress.co.nz

For information about bulk purchases,
please contact The Copy Press, Bookshop.

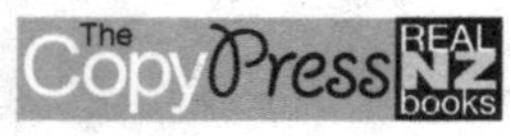

Contents

ONE

Louise

1992

A KID OF about five came to her doorstep on a scooter. 'Have you seen Rashid?' he asked. It was nearly dark and the boy's sixteen-year-old brother had gone missing after school the night before. A few minutes later a policeman arrived. The headmaster had suggested Louise Hammond be paid a visit. Yes, she was a friend of the Indian couple who ran the corner grocery store, but she didn't buy the explanation.

This fine spring day had started with choir practice at the community hall. Choristers met every second Friday, except at Easter. Sessions with the choirmaster and pianist ran between nine and ten-thirty, followed by a morning tea. Louise never missed it. The girls at her shop had hastened their manageress away, saying how fabulous she looked. Louise was the first local to wear vintage fashions and took extra care on choir days. Frocks unearthed from their mothers' era tickled the older women.

'Come in, Sergeant,' she said, stepping back. 'And here is me in my pink dressing gown and fluffy slippers about to wash my hair.'

There were no knickers or hosiery hanging on the clothes horse beside the bay window. She had checked. Yet, Sergeant Ronald Winfield still looked uncomfortable standing in her living room. The man wasn't very broad-minded.

It wasn't the first time the teen had crept away from his family to be with his mates. As the officer droned on about the worried parents, asking who would pick up the potatoes and cabbages for the pub, Louise drifted into thoughts about her new life.

Two years ago she had moved to 9 Shepherds Lane in Limetree. The estate agent had been right. It *was* a 'picturesque country town'. Here she could find peace among the pastured fields, the vacant scrubland and forested hills. She'd heard rural people were more accepting. Frankly, she was tired of the city flimflam and prejudice. She had made mistakes. The antique shop she'd purchased in the village generated poor returns. Few customers were interested in its stock of old furniture

     Kayleen M. Hazlehurst

and bric-a-brac—glass vases, china teacups, porcelain figurines, painted miniatures and pre-loved jewellery. But by adding a range of vintage clothes, she had started to turn things around.

The sopranos and altos got behind her, bringing their out-of-date frocks into the shop, rather than taking them to the flea markets. Florals, pleats, polka dots and stripes. *Harper's Bazaar* panache. Treasures that made customers shriek when they found them.

She tossed off a little laugh. 'So we are on another hunt for the naughty Rashid, Sergeant?'

The policeman did a quick recce of the room. Majeed studied her with large black eyes and smiled when he heard the word 'naughty'.

'What about you, Majeed?' she asked. 'Any idea where your brother is?'

He dolefully shook his head.

'Did Mum ask you to fetch me?'

The boy nodded.

Winfield seemed impatient to get home to his dinner. A member of the choir himself, he would turn up on occasions to exercise his baritone vocal cords.

'I didn't see you at the hall this morning,' Louise said.

'Didn't I tell you? I was out looking for a lost teenager.'

'Sorry, he's not here. Would you like me to talk to Mr and Mrs Bashi? Take this one back to his parents?' She tilted her head towards the child.

'I can drive you, if you like. You okay with walking home?'

'Main Street is well lit,' she answered.

'By the way, where were you today?'

'After choir I went to the shop. Where else would I be?'

'Anyone see you?'

'Don't be ridiculous, Ronny. Of course they did.'

'Just doing my job ... Don't leave town without telling me.'

She lifted her shoulders in a sigh. 'Why would I leave? I have a business to run.'

Some months earlier her assistants, Jenny and Gail, had concocted the idea of a boutique café. A tearoom with a bric-a-brac ambience. Louise liked the idea. Home cooking with Mum had filled many happy hours of childhood. There was enough money to install a modest kitchen and she let the eatery flow through the shop.

The old standbys of bangers and mash, sausage rolls, pie and peas, and fish and chips were put on the menu for any stray men, but the main attractions for women were the finger sandwiches, smoked fish savouries, devilled eggs and a selection of 'Grandma's sweet treats'. High teas were back in vogue.

A TV special showcased Louise's Vintage Café and

Kayleen M. Hazlehurst

overnight Limetree became 'charming'. Friends came to exchange recipes and to share tiny versions of melting moments, chocolate Afghans, Madeira cake and scones with strawberry jam and cream. In keeping with the theme, a few ladies wore fifties twinsets with flared skirts and rayon scarves. Tourists who stopped in for the new eating experience went on to explore the local shops. It had been good for the whole town and the sergeant knew it.

Louise tightened her dressing gown and edged towards the hall. 'Give me a minute to dress.'

'I'll meet you at the car. Come on, kid. How would you like a ride in a police car?'

She raked through her bedroom closet. Parents of a lost child required something sedate and she settled on the dark-blue linen. A Betty Carol fold-over with large buttons. She adjusted her wig in the long mirror and ran her hands over her slim hips. At forty-two she wasn't frumpy. She drew on her coat, hesitating before discarding the pearl brooch.

During the drive she told the policeman which songs the choir had practised that morning, neither adult wanting to discuss their worst fears in front of an anxious little boy.

'We did a bit of scat. Listened to a tape of Ella Fitzgerald and Mel Tormé. It was fun.'

Ronny shook his head. 'I'm sorry I missed that.'

Boy and scooter were dismounted on the pavement outside Bashi's Groceries.

'Thanks for the lift,' Louise said. 'I'll let you know if I learn anything.' Immigrant families were not keen on talking to the police, even about misplaced relatives.

A lady in a blue sari and white apron, looking all of her fortyish years, came to the front step. She appeared relieved to see them but presented a stern face. 'Majeed, I asked you to bring me Louise, not to bother the policeman for a ride home.'

'That was my fault,' Louise said. 'Majeed and Sergeant Winfield arrived at my house about the same time. He offered us a ride and I accepted. Hope you don't mind.'

The woman shrugged. 'Dinner is in the kitchen, Majeed. Hurry now, Dad will need your help.' She waved them inside, then asked Louise, 'Why was the policeman visiting?'

'He's been making enquiries. I'm sure he thinks I'm hiding Rashid in my back room ... Silly man.'

'Well, we don't think you are. Come in, dear. We must talk.'

'Have you heard anything yet?'

'Nothing.' Mrs Bashi lifted her apron to wipe her eyes.

 Kayleen M. Hazlehurst

'They think Rashid has run away, but we fear someone has stolen him.'

'Goodness.' She was ushered into the family room behind the kitchen.

'You will take us seriously, won't you, Louise?'

'Certainly, I will. Has someone been threatening you?'

'We'll wait for Sabat. Can I offer you a cup of tea? It's my special blend.'

'That would be wonderful, Mrs Bashi.'

'Please, call me Aesha. I have prepared samosas. Fried vegetable dumplings. Do you like them?'

Louise removed her coat. 'I love anything Indian.'

Tea came on a trolley with matching cups and teapot. 'Next time you must come to dinner. That's a nice dress. What is the material?'

'Linen. You can touch the fabric if you like. I put it on when I can't think of anything else to wear.'

Aesha's eyelashes fluttered, as if she was struggling with a question. 'Have you always worn women's clothes?'

'I wore a three-piece suit to my office in Auckland.'

'Your job must have been very important.'

'I was a financial adviser. Sadly, I saw the worst of humanity in that work. There's too much greed in the city.'

Aesha stopped pouring their tea. 'So, you moved

to Limetree and became a woman?' she said, her voice rising slightly.

Louise brooded for a moment, then went on. 'When I was a child, my sister, Kimberly, used to dress me up like a doll. I liked the attention. She could be cruel when I looked like a boy. I guess she wanted a little sister.'

'That was very unfair.'

'I have cross-dressed on and off most of my life.'

'Well, I don't see the harm.'

'Some people don't like me because of it.'

'Never mind. People don't like us because of the colour of our skin, or our religion, or because our clothes are different.'

'I'm sorry. That must be painful.'

'In India we embraced our differences. Our lives were much more vibrant and colourful.'

'I understand.' Louise knew the need for vibrancy and colour.

'In Kerala, the state we are from, Hindu men dress as women during the Kottankulangara Festival in honour of the goddess, Bhagavathy. A thousand men put on make-up and their brightest saris to please the goddess and to seek her blessings.' Aesha smiled. 'Oh Louise, I wish you could see them …'

Mr Bashi came in and crumpled into the chair beside her.

     Kayleen M. Hazlehurst

'Long day?' Louise asked.

'I've been up since five. How are you, my dear? Your business is flourishing?'

'I've made some progress.'

'Good. We all benefit when our neighbours prosper.'

'I've been telling her about the temple festival, Sabat.'

'Ah, yes. The night when ordinary men are transformed into demure goddesses, each bringing to the temple their own offerings and sacredness. It's a wonderful ceremony. Crowds visit Kerala for the festival. There is always an elephant.'

Louise laughed. 'Only in India ...'

'Sabat was a supplicant before we were married.'

'Why, Aesha, I think you are blushing.'

Aesha's smile was coy. 'Some devotees are very beautiful.'

Louise sat forward to sip her tea. 'And many devotees are young men?'

'Yes,' Aesha said softly.

'May I ask what blessings you beseeched from your Devi, Sabat?'

'I was seeking a wife and good fortune.'

'As young men do.'

Aesha glanced over as she attended to Sabat. 'When you are not Louise, what is your name? What did your mother call you?'

'She named me Lewis.'

'And sometimes you dress as a man?'

Louise chuckled. 'When I'm washing my car.'

Sabat lowered his cup and wiped his moustache. 'I should like to meet this Lewis fellow. Does he like fishing?'

'Not particularly, but he'll watch a game of cricket with you.'

It was late before she got away from her friends. The small talk about cross-dressing goddesses was intriguing, with or without the elephant, but what interested her most were the couple's thoughts about their lost son and why they expected to hear something soon.

To get home she had to walk past a row of small shops and The Ploughman, a traditional country pub. *If only I'd brought my wheels.*

She had two vehicles. An '86 Holden Gemini she'd bought cheaply in Auckland before the model was discontinued, and a dishevelled truck she'd inherited with the antique shop. She enjoyed driving the battered pickup—the way every bump and curve in the road tethered her to the environment.

Even with her coat wrapped tight, her heart pounded and her ankles wobbled in her heels as catcalls and taunts were hurled at her by drunken patrons outside the hotel.

'Hello, darling, want a date? I'm available.'

Louise heard men laughing, and an engine revving-up as she hurried away. She turned onto the dim path leading to Shepherds Lane, avoiding the dark driveways and hedges. Those men at the pub knew who she was. Many had come to the café to stare at her during the day. By the time she got home she was shaking.

On Saturday afternoon she visited the police station.

'You must make Rashid your top priority, Sergeant. People are getting twitchy.'

Neville and Lance, two young constables at their desks, pretended not to be listening.

'That's what I'm doing,' Ronald whispered over the counter. 'Anyway, what do you know about runaway kids?'

'More than you think. And he may not be a runaway.'

The policeman regarded her with cool grey eyes. 'Maybe one of *your* folk grabbed him?'

'What do you mean *my* folk?'

He tipped his head three times and smirked.

Louise gave him a silent glare.

Winfield turned red. 'Never mind. Auckland Central have a photo. They will be trawling the city, checking out the streets and sleazy clubs.'

'Rashid could have joined an Indian dancing troupe.

He might be heading for Bollywood as we speak.'

'Oh, I doubt ...' Winfield raised his eyebrows. 'Really?'

'It's one of the parents' theories. Have you considered looking closer to home? I don't feel safe here at the moment, myself. A few men have been getting nasty.'

'What do you expect?' He waved his hand over her dress.

'So I'm the architect of some boy-snatching ring between Limetree and Auckland?'

'You said it, not me ... Are you?'

'I don't have any criminal leanings, Ronny. But you already know that.'

'Yeah, I've checked you out. Sorry those bastards have been bothering you.' He looked apologetic ... 'I have a dog.'

'What?'

'Useless thing, sent to me last week from the Police Dog Section. Spectacular dropout from training school. Frightened of his own shadow.'

'What are you saying?'

'The mutt needs a home ... You need protection ... How about taking him in until I get something sorted?'

She paused. 'Is the animal friendly?'

'Love ya to death. Too nice for police work. Doesn't want a bar of chasing villains, hates searching for drugs, and is none too keen on cadaver detection.'

 Kayleen M. Hazlehurst

'I don't blame him... I suppose I could take him to the café.'

Neville lifted his head. 'You won't have to buy a thing.'

Lance got to his feet. 'I could drop him off with his stuff before dinner.'

'How much stuff?'

'Just a bed and a few toys.'

'All right. I'll give your wretched dog a home until you find Rashid. As long as you lot put your backs into the search.'

'Teamwork. That's the spirit.' The sergeant almost sounded like he believed his own rhetoric.

She turned to go, feeling railroaded. Glancing back, she saw the whole station had come up smiles. 'What kind of dog is it?'

'Black Labrador.'

'Bit of a sook but has a bark like a foghorn.'

'Would scare away any prowler.'

'Thanks a bunch.'

Winfield held open the door. 'I reckon Bentley will suit you down to the ground.'

'Bentley. That's his name?'

'Yeah.'

'Sounds enormous.'

The canine arrived an hour later with his paraphernalia, including two bowls and a box of dog food. Louise and the Labrador stood in the kitchen staring at each other. He was an impressive animal, about eighteen months old. Black coat, so shiny ducks could use him as a water slide. Solid neck and shoulders. Broad head. Not the sort of pet a lady in a pencil skirt should be seen towed along by. As his name suggested, Bentley was a finely-tuned machine who just wanted to run.

⟊

Lewis rose early and put on his jeans and pullover. After a man-sized Sunday breakfast for them both, he grabbed his mackintosh and boots from the porch.

'Come on, boy. Get in the truck.'

By the time he mounted the driver's seat, the dog was settled on the passenger side as if he owned the spot, with his eyes fixed straight ahead.

'There's a walk not far from here. You'll like it. A forest with lots of room to explore. You'd better behave, else it'll be the park from now on.'

Bentley lolloped his tongue around his lips, spraying saliva on the glove compartment.

'Lovely.' Lewis reached for a cloth to wipe the animal's mouth. 'I know, you're excited. Cooped up all week at the station, were you?'

 Kayleen M. Hazlehurst

They turned off the highway and continued on a side road for a few minutes before pulling into a carpark. A *Public Walkway* sign had been nailed to the gate post, accompanied by a map, and the request to *Please stay on the path.*

Lewis was familiar with Winchester Forest. A creek could be followed down to the road if a person got lost. He tightened the laces of his hiking boots and shouldered his rucksack. He had only packed emergency items—a medical kit, a knife and rope, a trowel and some toilet paper, a water bottle, supply of nuts and raisins, and two dog biscuits.

He had also brought one of Rashid's shirts provided by the boy's parents.

He had stopped in again at the corner store before Saturday closing.

'Hello, I'm Lewis.'

Aesha had taken a step back, this being the first time she'd seen him in men's clothing. Without the wig, he had short brown hair that was greying at the temples.

Sabat grasped his extended hand. 'Glad to meet you, Lewis. This is a very great pleasure.'

'Will you stay a while?' Aesha asked, having recovered herself.

'Sorry, not this evening. I have a house guest.'

After explaining he was caring for a rescue dog, the mother had rushed off to find an item of clothing.

'Get his sports shirt,' Sabat called after her. 'The one he kept in his school locker,' then he turned to Lewis. 'Will you do some detective work for us, my friend?'

Aesha came back from the bedroom in tears. 'Please, Lewis,' she begged as she handed over the shirt. 'Please help us find Rashid before it's too late.'

The forest park was always quiet on Sunday mornings. Bentley was scratching at the truck door to get out. The animal raced through the gate and left the path with Lewis following. After vanishing for a few minutes, Bentley rocketed back and bounced off his legs.

'Hey, watch it!'

The black dog dropped his bum into top gear and streaked off into a loop. Lewis trotted towards a stand of kauri and tōtara, wondering if he would ever see the animal again. High-pitched yelping indicated Ben had fastened onto a rabbit trail. There was no point trying to catch a speeding dog. Either the rabbit would outrun him or the trail would go cold. Lewis checked his watch and sat down on a log to wait. In a short time, he heard panting.

He whistled to the dark shape weaving through the trees. 'Over here, Ben. Come, boy.'

 Kayleen M. Hazlehurst

Bentley came padding towards him, carrying something in his mouth.

'What have you got there?'

As the dog neared him, he realised it was the frayed sleeve of a chequered shirt with the clawed bones of a hand.

Limetree Police Station called in reinforcements. Three experienced handlers with their detection dogs flew in via the airfield north of the town.

Lewis and Bentley showed the team the general area. They had scoured the forest earlier but *old Clueless* couldn't remember where he had found the bones. While the professionals did a wide sweep, Bentley whined and pulled at his lead.

'Quiet, boy. You had your chance.'

It was midday before the police located the human remains.

During a three hour search the bystanders at the entrance to the forest had grown to a small crowd. Clustered behind the orange tape, they wanted to know why murderers were burying bodies so near to their peaceful village.

The Bashis were assured the body could not have been their missing son. Decomposition confirmed the bones had lain there for some time, and Mrs Bashi said Rashid had never owned a chequered shirt. With no other missing persons on his books, Sergeant Winfield was at a loss to come up with an identity. 'Forensics should help us with that,' he muttered, shaking his head.

Auckland Central Police wanted to be sure no more bodies were buried in the park and the detection team was instructed to widen its search. Bentley was not invited to attend the next day. It was probably for the best. Being left out the first time had made the beast mopey.

❦

Louise read up on Labradors. Daily walks and games of fetch and tug-of-war were supposed to build confidence in a dog, but Ben had other problems. Fireworks, backfiring cars, being left alone for more than five minutes. A clap of thunder had him wedged behind a lounge chair with his pupils thrust sideways and the whites of his eyes reflecting spotlights off the ceiling.

From his behaviour it was clear Ben was empathetic. At the café he would lick a crying child or nuzzle a sad grown-up. If they were ever burgled, Louise was certain Bentley would help the thief carrying out the silverware.

One speculation about Rashid's disappearance kept

     Kayleen M. Hazlehurst

circling back. In any domestic situation a relative was often suspected and it came to light that Sabat had a disgruntled older brother, who had arrived in New Zealand on the same wave of migration.

Zahir owned a successful Indian restaurant in central Auckland. Aesha and Sabat were particularly reticent when speaking about Rashid's uncle, and his rise to affluence. Louise guessed he dealt in more than curries. Maybe his booths were convenient places for seedier transactions. Businessmen with their fingers in the wrong pots, money laundering, get-rich-quick schemes, illegal gambling, prostitution and the growing drug trade. While one shady relative in the city might not hurt an honest, hard-working couple with a small country store, this landscape suddenly changed when she discovered Zahir bore a grudge.

The family story had come out on the Friday night. Back in Kerala the first wife of the older brother had died young, having failed to bear him a son. Three years later he and his second wife were afflicted by similar misfortune. Some time before the two families migrated, the second sister-in-law gave birth at the same maternity hospital as Aesha. Sons were born hours apart to the two women.

During the night one child passed away. Zahir berated the nursery. Maddened with grief, he alleged they had switched babies. There was a bitter struggle and the stricken father had to be dragged away by police. He had never forgiven Sabat and Aesha.

Relating the event, Aesha had lifted her hands in an appeal to Louise. 'Rashid will be seventeen next month. If his uncle offers him a job, and he accepts, the authorities will never challenge it.'

'Our son would never be seduced by Zahir's riches,' Sabat insisted. 'He's being held against his will. Now the boy is grown my brother thinks he can steal him from us. He has been plotting this for years.'

These were wild ideas, yet they sounded plausible. 'Would Zahir have kidnapped the boy himself?'

Sabat rammed down his fist. 'You can bet he sent others to do his dirty work.'

'They took Rashid on his way home from school,' Aesha sobbed. 'He'll be so frightened.'

'Then it is definitely abduction. No matter what age he is. Do you want me to tell the police?'

Sabat shifted forward. 'The kidnappers will cut his throat if we involve the police!'

Aesha uttered a cry and put her hand to her mouth.

'Don't worry,' Louise had said, reaching out her hand. 'I'll make some discreet enquiries. It's amazing what people will tell you over a cup of coffee and a free lump of coconut ice.'

 Kayleen M. Hazlehurst

The police were conducting their enquiries house to house. It wasn't every day a child in school uniform was snatched off the streets of Limetree. Rashid would have resisted. There'd have been a struggle.

Louise's first port of call was the café. At closing time, she told Jenny and Gail about her mission to find the missing youth and the girls swung right in behind her.

'We must recruit the choir ladies,' Gail said, as she washed the last dishes.

Jenny tidied away the cups. 'Should we invite them for morning tea?'

'I don't see why not.' Louise agreed, a meeting was the quickest way to launch an investigation. 'We'll make extra pikelets.'

Jenny collapsed into giggles against the sink. 'Twenty old ducks asking around will unearth more information than those police officers ever can.'

'Don't let Sergeant Winfield hear you say that.'

'Sergeant Winfield couldn't find his necessities on his wedding night,' Gail said dryly, sending them screeching into the next room to straighten the tables.

The choir ladies arrived at 10 am. Each had expressed a concern for the Bashi family and a morning tea was an excellent opportunity for a natter. Three of the women had sons in produce delivery. Two daughters catered for the school. There were friends who were daily shoppers. Grandchildren, too, had sharp eyes. They would ask if anyone had seen anything suspicious—a lurking vehicle, men acting funny.

After work, while they waited for incoming intelligence, Louise and Bentley went to hunt for clues. Their strolls between the corner store and the school gates produced nothing. She stopped at the hairdresser's for the latest gossip, then the bakery where local children bought doughnuts, all to no avail.

Cruising homeward in the truck she tried to imagine where criminals might lie low for three or four days. The police were doing spot-checks along the highway. Nearby farms were on the alert. The sea required a boat, but coastal destinations had many eyes.

That only left ... 'The airfield, Ben! Why didn't I think of it?'

Bentley answered with a resounding 'Woo-woo' and sloshed his tongue round his lips.

Lewis threw his wig on the seat, wiped off his lipstick, and did a one-eighty outside the police station. He took out his mobile phone, although he still hadn't got used to using the clunky brick.

 Kayleen M. Hazlehurst

'I know where they are, Jenny. I'm going out to the airfield. Can you tell Gail?'

'Look for a van with two men,' was her urgent response. 'That's what the ladies are saying. Plain white. No signs or markings.'

'Right.'

There were two more hours of daylight. Plenty of time to reach the site before sunset. Further north, the unmanned strip was being used by recreational pilots, aerial top dressers, medical helicopters and for police emergencies.

As he neared the turn-off, he glanced at the highway through his rear-view mirror. On the range he could see flashing lights. The girls had alerted the police. A dark line of other vehicles trailed behind. It looked like half the population of Limetree was coming to the rescue.

'Damn it!'

Lewis turned onto the gravel road and stopped. He snatched up his T-shirt and jeans from the back seat, changed his clothes, and shoved his feet into a solid pair of sandshoes.

When he reached the airfield, he stopped to check for human activity. A cluster of storage units and sheds stood at the edge of the strip. Parked outside one was an unmarked white van.

'Gotcha!'

'*Mm-m-m-m,*' said Bentley.

Lewis slipped the truck into gear, estimating he had ten minutes before the cavalry arrived. As the truck rolled forward, its tyres scrunching over the stony ground, the dog became tense.

'Okay, boy,' he said, reaching under his seat to retrieve Rashid's shirt. 'Sniff this.'

As he drew in behind the building a deep rumble emitted from Bentley's chest. Either the dog didn't like the situation, or he'd caught a scent.

'Good boy. Stay here.'

Lewis crept to the corner of the shed and crouched down. In the window facing the airfield he saw a flickering light, perhaps a candle. Two men were conversing rapidly in what he guessed was Hindi and a younger voice was answering in English.

'No. I want to go home!'

'Shut your mouth!'

He heard a crack and a thump. Someone had been hit. Had fallen. The boy was calling for his mother, making Lewis clench his fists.

Out of the crimson clouds came the buzz of a descending aircraft. A sliding door scraping on metal was his cue to depart. He rolled to the side and darted behind the shed. Small planes could land, turn around, and take off in minutes. This one was already lining up its headlights.

 Kayleen M. Hazlehurst

In the seconds it took Lewis to get back into his pickup, the men had bundled a blanketed figure out of the shed and were running with him across the field.

'Hang on, Ben. This will be rough.'

He spun the vehicle onto the grass. The kidnappers were just yards from the plane, shouting to each other as the truck bore down on them. They shoved their victim on board while the pilot revved the engines and reset the wing flaps.

As the aircraft started to move the last thing Lewis saw was Rashid's desperate face at the plane window. Something inside him broke, seeing that boy so overpowered.

'Agh-h-h!'

Lewis dropped a gear and booted the accelerator, sending up a cloud of dust. He pelted along the airstrip until he was parallel with the horrified face of the pilot. Lewis smiled coolly, drew his finger across his neck, and pointed for the plane to pull over.

Behind him a racket had broken out as police and other vehicles joined in the chase. Sirens, and twenty carloads of screaming citizens were too much for Bentley. The dog stuck his head out the window and bayed like a basset hound.

The pilot didn't call his bluff, seeing the maniac beside him was about to throw a truck under his wheels.

The plane coughed and slowed to a halt as the police and the rest of the snarling pack surrounded it like a cornered hog.

The parents came over as the police led three men away in handcuffs.

Aesha was in tears. 'Oh, thank you, dear. Thank you.' The dazed youngster beside her nodded vigorously.

Sabat gripped Lewis' hand. 'May all the goddesses smile their blessings on your life, my dear friend.'

Gail and Jenny with a group of fascinated locals watched on.

Jenny placed her hand on his chest. 'Lewis, eh?' She grinned. 'Don't you scrub up lovely?'

The Magic Comb

THINGS WERE QUIET again. As they approached Christmas there were no more policemen knocking on doors making enquiries, no more rumblings of discontent about 'city villains' burying bodies in local forests, no more rudeness to passing ladies from the men at the pub. Sergeant Winfield had given them a sorting out. 'Louise may be a weirdo, but she's our weirdo,' he'd told them.

Each day the children walked safely to school, the lucky ones returning from Cooper's Bakery with their jam doughnuts and creamy pastry-horns. Louise's Vintage Café, a favourite place for high teas, was as busy as ever with their new and returning customers.

All seemed peaceful at Limetree—except for the heart of a little girl.

When Louise saw the young one poking among the jewellery trays in her shop, trying to be inconspicuous, she recognised a troubled soul. The girl was not much older than eight.

'Can I help you, dear?'

'Oh, yes. Thank you.'

'Are we looking for something special? A pretty brooch for Granny or a necklace for Mum? Is it for a birthday?'

The girl straightened herself. 'Mum said I must introduce myself to people. My name is Angela.'

'I am very pleased to meet you, Angela. You can call me Louise.' She extended her hand and received a feathery handshake in return. 'Do you know what you are you seeking or do you want a few ideas?'

The girl sighed. 'I've been looking everywhere for a magic comb.'

Louise pulled out a chair by a table. 'Well, now. A magic comb. This will indeed need some thought. Sit here while I get you a glass of milk from the kitchen. Then you can tell me why we are looking for such a precious thing.'

'Thank you.'

'Won't be a moment ... How about a chocolate strawberry?'

Angela brightened. 'That would be nice.'

 Kayleen M. Hazlehurst

It was almost 4 o'clock. Jenny and Gail were clearing tables and saying goodbye to their last customers as Louise returned with the milk.

'I warmed it for you,' she said as she placed the glass on the table, along with two strawberries coated with sweet dark chocolate. 'Children are always hungry after school. Where is Mum?'

'She gets back from work in an hour. I came here straight from school.'

Louise tut-tutted. 'I see. She thinks you're at home doing your homework? Perhaps you should explain to me why it's so important to find a magic comb.'

Angela blinked her brown eyes and a small tear slid down her cheek. 'Mum is so sad. Every night she cries herself to sleep. She thinks I don't know, but I hear her through the vent between our rooms.'

'Why is Mum sad?'

'Daddy went over the sea and he hasn't come back.'

'What do you mean, over the sea?'

There was a long pause as the girl struggled to compose her answer.

Louise bent closer. 'Is he a fisherman? Does he work for a cruise ship? Or is it the Navy?'

'Mum says he's an adventurer. He goes out in boats to rescue people from pirates and bad men.'

'An adventurer.' Louise smiled. 'An interesting line of

work. So, he hasn't returned from his adventuring and this has made Mum cry?'

Angela turned to scan the shop's bric-a-brac on the shelves against the wall, then she lowered her gaze.

'Don't worry, dear.' Louise said. 'On Saturdays we have a special morning tea for mothers and daughters. Come together and we can have a cup of tea and a chat. What is Mum's name?'

'Ellie Brownlea. She works at the doctor's rooms.'

Jenny and Gail had joined them, listening with interest.

'Oh, I know Ellie,' Gail said. 'She's the receptionist.'

'A nice lady,' Jenny confirmed. 'We promise to keep our eyes peeled for your special comb. Is it to cheer up your mother?'

'No, it's for me.'

Louise tilted her head. 'So you can—?'

'So I can turn myself into a mermaid and find Dad.'

'Ah. You have been reading the story of the little mermaid.'

'Mum has been reading it to me.'

'And if you comb your lovely locks with the mermaid comb you can swim across the wild sea, brave the wicked pirates, and bring Dad home. Is that it?'

Angela reached to stroke the café's sympathetic dog, who had his head against her knee. 'I know it sounds silly.'

 Kayleen M. Hazlehurst

Louise leaned back on her chair. 'On the contrary, I think it is a noble objective for a caring daughter. If you want something special you've come to the right place, hasn't she, girls?'

'That's right,' declared Jenny. 'We are an antique shop, after all.'

'Woo-woo', the Labrador concurred and licked the girl's hand.

Gail laughed. 'There, you see. Even Bentley agrees. There's nothing we like more than a treasure hunt.'

Louise needed to do a little research. Fair skies had clouds, but she'd learnt they could be dispersed with a brisk gust of information. If this father and husband had been kept from his family there was probably a good reason. Friday was choir day and she would start by talking with her friend and fellow chorister, Sergeant Winfield.

The choir was preparing for its Christmas concert to be held Sunday fortnight on the quadrangle, while the school hosted its annual Pet Day. Summer holidays were almost upon them and the children were getting excited. Parents were invited to donate vegetables, home baked goods, and preserves for the fundraising stalls. Louise's café had promised them a chocolate banana cake.

All twenty members of the choir were assembled at the hall. Louise was put between the altos and the tenors, as usual. This was so she could decide where to pitch her voice. The choir was short in the lower registers, and here she could sing with unbridled spirit. Her unique talent was never wasted.

After an hour on their Christmas repertoire—*God Rest Ye Merry Gentlemen, Away in a Manger, We Wish You a Merry Christmas*—someone suggested they jazz things up a bit with Mel Tormé's *Chestnuts Roasting on an Open Fire*, and Bing Crosby's *White Christmas*. They had practised for forty minutes and soon everyone was standing around, enjoying a cup of tea, when Louise edged over to the policeman to ask her question.

'Ellie Brownlea's husband?' the sergeant responded. 'Yes, I know Adam.'

'Have you had word of him lately?' Louise asked.

'I heard he was in some kind of UN peacekeeping operation. He'd been assigned to a coastal patrol team helping refugees escape by boat from Vietnam into Cambodia.'

'Sounds dangerous. Would the navy be keeping an eye on things?'

'Those lads would be on their own once they headed into these territories. Though there might be one of our frigates hovering in open waters they could call on.'

 Kayleen M. Hazlehurst

'Any chance of a mission like this going wrong? Would we hear anything?'

'They keep things pretty quiet … Who's asking?'

'Adam's daughter. Her mother is mad with worry. I'm meeting them at the café in the morning and want to give them some news.'

'I know one or two higher-ups in the navy. Want me to make some enquiries?'

'Thanks, Ronald. That would be helpful.'

'I'll try to shake things up a bit. Tell them we need some intel. The police and military often work together. I guess I owe you that after the last palaver. How's Bentley?'

'Doing well. You want him back?'

Winfield laughed. 'I'd rather he stayed with you.'

'Thought you might.' Louise smiled. 'As it turns out, Bentley's a good helping dog. It's funny how he knows when a person is sad. Makes a beeline straight for them.'

'A helping dog! Huh, that's a new one. Perhaps we should train Labradors. Give them certificates.' He shook his head. 'A therapy dog, eh? Doubt that will ever take off.'

Mother and daughter morning teas, which ran on Saturday between nine-thirty and eleven, were becoming popular. Jenny and Gail looked smart in their shop-girl outfits—black dresses with lace collars, cobbled together from Louise's 1950s collection. They loved the way mothers made a fuss of the younger children with best dresses and hair ribbons. The older girls who had Saturday sports either didn't attend or wore their gym skirts and tops. Some genuine bonding was going on over the cheese fingers and miniature teacakes. Everyone seemed hungry and the chatter was incessant.

Louise reserved a small table in a corner next to the kitchen. Ellie and Angela arrived early, explaining they could only stay for an hour as Angela had netball.

'I'm so glad you came,' Louise said, as she placed a plate of savoury and sweet selections on the table. How are you both?'

Ellie looked embarrassed. 'I'm sorry my daughter has bothered you with our problems,' she said. 'She really shouldn't have.'

'Oh no, dear. Who wouldn't be anxious in your situation?'

Ronald Winfield had called Louise early that morning. It was true, Adam Brownlea was working with the navy in the Gulf of Thailand. The team's surveillance work of the rivers and coasts was critical to UN efforts to bring democracy to Cambodia. She'd been instructed not to go into details, but she could give some assurance to the family.

 Kayleen M. Hazlehurst

'Have you been able to find out anything?' the wife asked Louise.

'Communications have been interrupted for a while, but we managed to get through a message that you and your daughter were worried. From what we heard, your husband and his friends are still engaged in their important mission.'

'My husband is safe?'

'Yes, Mrs Brownlea. Last night the navy made radio contact with one of their agents on land. A villager paddled out to check on the patrol launch. There is nothing untoward to report. Everyone is well. Their radio gear has been repaired. The team just need more time to complete their tasks. You should be hearing from your husband very soon.'

Mother and daughter hugged each other, their tears and words of joy drowned out by the hubbub of the tearoom.

Jenny came to the kitchen door, looking desperate.

'Please excuse me, I'm needed in the galley,' Louise said. 'But before I slip away, I have something special for Angela.'

She reached into her apron pocket and pulled out a delicately carved piece of tortoise shell, with tiny diamantes along its rim.

'Just in case,' she whispered as she pressed the magic comb into the girl's hand.

THREE

Basil and the Golden Calf

EVERYONE KNEW BASIL the black cat, who was best friends with Wally the calf. They were both special animals. Wally, with the pale honey coat of the Jersey breed. Basil, with the short-haired astuteness of the farm moggy, kept for his ratting abilities.

Wally was really a girl, and her name should have been Wallerene according to young Sam McGee. Except Sam much preferred the masculine version. So Wally it was, teats and all.

Sam was explaining this to Louise when she came early to deliver her chocolate banana cake to the school stall. Pet Day was a much-loved event when every variety of clawed, hooved or woolly friend was invited to attend Limetree Primary School. The pet parade on the playing field would be followed by the bestowal of red, blue or yellow ribbons, in accordance with the judges' criteria for animal excellence and the orderliness of child and beast.

Louise had noticed the dangling bare legs of the boy in brown shorts on the stone wall at the entrance. Eleven-year-old Sam looked forlorn as he watched the stream of children and pets arrive at the school.

'All alone, Sam? I thought you'd have Wally with you.'

'Wally has disappeared.'

'Gosh. How?'

'Thieves. A bunch of sheep were taken from our front paddock. Twenty ewes, Dad reckons. Nicked from right under our noses. There were tyre tracks in the paddock.'

Though rare, sheep rustlers had been known to drive to an isolated farm and melt into the night with a haul of livestock.

'What happened?'

'My calf sleeps in the paddock with the sheep. The thieving buggers must have snatched her as well.'

'Oh Sam, I'm so sorry.' Louise could see the boy was close to tears.

'This morning when I got up Dad was yelling and Mum was telling him not to swear. The baby was screaming her head off. Then Dad slammed the door and took off in the Land Rover and Mum was standing by the door crying ... I'm just a kid, I dunno what to do.'

 Kayleen M. Hazlehurst

Clyde McGee had a short fuse when things went wrong. With hefty mortgages and loans to pay, finances for small farmers were stretched. Being robbed blind could drive an honest man into self-loathing, feeling he should have prevented the misfortune. They were often too proud to report the crimes. Louise felt sorry for the whole family and thought she'd better stop in later with a basket of scones.

'Poor Sam. Pet Day without your pet. What about Basil? I thought that cat loved Wally.'

'Basil's gone too. I'm sure he slipped onto the truck to protect Wally. Those sheep stealers don't know what they're in for. Basil can be mean.'

'I'm sure. Basil could beat up my Bentley any day.'

Sam looked down and smiled. 'Your Bentley's a wuss of a dog.'

'I know.' She laughed. 'Anyway, it wouldn't hurt to tell Sergeant Winfield in case the thieves plan to rob someone else.' She looked around and saw the rest of the Limetree Choir arriving. 'Sorry Sam, I have to join my friends for our concert.' She paused and looked intently at the boy. 'Get Dad to report this to the police. That's your best chance of getting back your pets.'

She placed her cake on the table next to Elsie McKay's onion jam and hurried away to the podium where the choir was assembling. Their task was to conjure up a jolly atmosphere until the headmistress was ready to welcome everyone. It was going to be a noisy and chaotic day.

❦

Sunday morning Lewis was outside washing his car when Ronald Winfield rolled up.

'Sergeant.'

'Ah, Lewis. I was hoping to see you.'

'Is this a social call?' The policeman was not in uniform.

'You could say that.'

'Come in. I'll make coffee. Did you enjoy yesterday?'

'I could have done without the animals.'

'That's not a nice way to speak of our children.'

Ronald guffawed, then he told Lewis that Clyde McGee had telephoned the station to report his missing sheep. 'I believe you had something to do with that.'

'No, that would be down to young Sam.'

'It's a low thing to steal a man's stock. Hitting farmers where it hurts.'

Lewis put out four Afghans, poured their coffee, and placed their mugs on a tray to take outside. 'There's a bit of sun on the balcony.'

Bentley rushed over with a tennis ball in his mouth.

Ronald smiled. 'Gidday, fella. You look settled in.'

     Kayleen M. Hazlehurst

They positioned two chairs beside the glass-topped table.

'Why can't the police catch them?'

Ronald shifted in his chair. 'This sort of crime … it's difficult to prove. Stolen animals often go unreported. Take McGee for example. He wakes up one morning and sees his son's pet calf has gone. Then he notices a hole in his flock and can only guess how many sheep have been taken.'

'If it wasn't for the missing calf he mightn't have noticed right away?'

'That's right. Trouble is, animal identification is a nightmare and so is the paperwork. Police tracing methods are poor and unless we can catch the culprit red-handed the courts are not impressed. The evidence is probably butchered and in freezers by lunchtime.'

'Walk me through it.' Lewis had encountered some slippery customers during his previous career in finance, but sheep stealing was something else. 'How do they do it?'

'You can never predict when or where they will strike. Rustlers have a fair bit of cunning. They round up the stock in the dark, drive them up a ramp, and take off without waking the farm dogs. Their vehicles are nondescript. Small trucks mostly. Some of those thieves have the skills of bloody Jock McKenzie's ghost.'

Lewis tilted his head in acknowledgement. 'So, they'd have experience with animals?'

'Yeah. Could even be shepherds.'

'Is this a class war, Ronald? The hungry barbarians swooping down on the wealthier farmers in the south?'

'I don't think the northerners are that hungry, Lewis. They can always go fishing or pig hunting.'

'Okay, here's another theory. Could sheep rustling be a way of restocking poorer farms? What you can't afford to buy, you steal in modest enough quantities not to seriously rattle the police?'

'Makes sense, though the reasons are murky.'

'Can't the government develop a better programme for struggling pastoralists? A bit more positive intervention and this problem might go away.'

'Sounds fancy. Anyway, our job is to stop the blighters from ripping the guts out of our farming community.'

'Is there anything I can do?'

Ronald stared down the back yard to the vegetable garden. 'You've got a fine plot there, Lewis.'

'My garden provides most of the veggies I need.'

'What the police need is hard evidence,' Ronald went on, as if talking to himself. 'Now, if there was someone who could go undercover ... Ask around without drawing attention ... ' He turned back to Lewis with a wily smile. 'A master of disguises. Know anyone like that?'

 Kayleen M. Hazlehurst

Lewis stroked Bentley's head and threw the tennis ball for the dog before answering. 'Will I get paid?'

Louise put on her blonde wig and manageress two-piece and left early for work. She intended to ask the girls at the café to look out for a man's leather coat.

Jenny fossicked through the antique clothing rack and located a World War II bomber jacket, complete with vintage goggles and a white aviator scarf.

'I don't know, Jenny. I'm not going to fly a Spitfire.'

'You want a longer jacket?'

'Yes. Something to protect my body. I might be buying a motorcycle.'

'Good grief.'

'I know, sorry.'

Gail butted in. 'My brother has a black leather jacket he hasn't worn for a decade. Too fat for it now. Likes his puddings.'

'Would he sell it to me if I threw in a chocolate cake?'

Bentley hopped onto the spare seat and adopted his intense stare on the road as Lewis swung the pickup from the driveway. He had always wanted to own a Harley-Davidson. Outside Bashi's Groceries a photograph of a 1984 model for sale was pinned to the noticeboard. He would have to drive to the Far North to have a look at the eight-year-old machine.

A person should never arrive at a new place empty handed and Dargaville was a good place to buy kūmara. A couple of sacks might come in handy when striking up conversations. He could pretend he was selling the sweet potatoes cheap. It wasn't only women who liked to gossip, so did old men. Especially if the attention of an interested stranger made them feel important.

The plan was to drive through the towns along the highway, stopping off at pubs and garages. He could buy a newspaper, visit the shops. Someone must have heard whispers about stolen sheep. Near Whangārei he pulled in at a motel by a park. People were gathering outside the fish and chip shop. After Bentley had been exercised and fed, he took a stroll.

In the morning he resolved to push on. The residents were too far south to know anything. Nothing fruitful was going to come from further enquiries. He figured the thieves would put a hundred or more kilometres between themselves and the farmers they stole from.

The following night he made camp outside Umawera,

 Kayleen M. Hazlehurst

on the upper reaches of Hokianga Harbour. Here beside the river he gave Bentley free range on a long rope tied to the open door of the truck. The dog preferred to sleep on the seat where he could guard the vehicle, but also keep an eye on his master in the tent.

Dinner was a shared tin of beef and vegetable stew. The baked beans would be saved for breakfast. Lewis slept the sleep of the just, in spite of the hard ground. There was enough warmth in his sleeping bag to let him drift away with his hand curled around the ragged tea-towel he'd used to lift the pot from the fire. Waking close to four, he lounged on the grass outside the tent, listening to the cicadas and staring up at the stars. The whimpers and groans of a dreaming dog drifted down to him. It was comforting, even though Lewis didn't mind his own company.

Dawn brought the musky scent of a rising tide as it covered the mudflats. In the new light the river became alive. Two white herons poked about on their spindly legs, looking for rock shrimps and crabs. A splash in the main channel indicated the presence of sprats or trevally. Among the mangroves he saw the cloudy disturbance of a flounder and the occasional fin of a parore as it grazed on seagrass.

A breeze carried the distant music from a car radio, then it faded, reminding him it was time to move on.

Kaitāia, the largest town on State Highway 1, was about 160 km northwest of Whangārei. At Kaitāia he would make his phone call about the motorbike. His destination was a settlement further north.

The map showed Waipapakauri sitting at the isthmus of the Aupōuri Peninsula, about twelve kilometres north of Kaitāia. From the hotel you could hear the surf of the Tasman Sea on the beach. The walls of the Waipapakauri Hotel were covered with photographs of the region's last 100 years of history. The room was cheap but clean, with a shared bathroom down the hall. A lounge restaurant offered him two courses. Meat and three veg with an option of soup or pud. Out back, there was a tavern where he hoped to meet a few locals over evening drinks.

The owner of the motorbike lived on a dusty metal road, midway between Waipapakauri and Kaitāia. Most of the area between the two settlements was farmland and Lewis imagined a fair bit would be under Māori ownership. One of the largest stations was managed by two families—one Māori and one Pākehā, after their intermarriage a century ago.

The appointment the next day to see the Harley was set for 10.30 am. As he drove there the December heat was starting to bite. Lewis reached to retrieve his

 Kayleen M. Hazlehurst

wide-brimmed hat and whacked it on his denims to remove the dust.

'Nearly there, boy. I'll give you a drink when we arrive.'

The dog gave Lewis' hand a slobbery lick and resumed his long-tongued panting.

A bearded man with greying hair to his shoulders waited outside a dilapidated farmhouse that hadn't seen a coat of paint in years. The front yard was littered with tyres, planks of wood, corrugated iron water tanks, damaged vehicles, trailers, toolboxes and a wooden chest filled with cow bells.

Lewis recognised the hint of an accent. *Could he be Swiss? That would explain the cow bells.* Kiwi cows wouldn't be seen dead wearing a cow bell. The man rested his hand proudly on the chassis of a magnificently restored, crimson and black, 1984 Harley-Davidson Low Rider.

After dispensing with the small talk the collector of things, who introduced himself merely as Luca, kicked off negotiations. 'The 1984 is a rare model,' he began. It turned out not only the cow bells had come out with him from Switzerland.

If his final price was accepted Luca said he would sweeten the deal. Three thousand dollars for the shiny motorcycle with a sidecar thrown in. A bundle of crisp banknotes and a handshake made them both happy. After some reshuffling, and the use of two planks as a ramp, the motorcycle and sidecar were loaded onto the back of the pickup.

'Have you got anything to cover them?' Luca asked.

'I've got an old tarp.'

'That'll do.'

They threw the tarpaulin over the bike and sidecar and tied it down with a rope.

'You can't be too careful,' Luca said, tactfully saying no more.

Lewis decided to stay another night at the hotel. He still didn't know who was doing the sheep rustling but was damn sure the locals would have some ideas. He would have a haircut in Kaitāia before heading back to Waipapakauri. Barber shops were good places for making enquiries.

He took a seat on a cracked red leather chair and noticed the mirror reflected a view of the street. Passers-by who glanced into Fred's Barber Shop lacked the hurried air of pedestrians in the city. The proprietor, Fred Penrose, drew a warm towel around Lewis' shoulders and plucked at his hair.

'Long on top … short back and sides?' Fred asked.

'Just a trim all over.'

 Kayleen M. Hazlehurst

'Shaved close?'

'Give it a little length. I burn in the sun.'

Fred tipped his head as if he understood the dangers of the northern sun to strangers. 'Are you visiting? I haven't seen you in these parts.'

Lewis closed his eyes while Fred sprayed his hair with water. 'I'm looking for work. Know any properties who are hiring?'

Fred worked in quick movements with his scissors, guided by a long comb. 'A few are shearing right now. Is that your truck outside?'

'Yeah.'

'What's under the tarp?'

Lewis paused. He guessed it was all right to lie while undercover. 'That's my posthole digger.'

'If it's farm work you want, I can suggest a couple of places.'

⁂

Eight dusty vehicles were scattered on the gravel drive-way. To his right, pens contained the sleek, snow-white bodies of the newly disrobed. As he stood by the entrance of a weather-worn shearing shed he could hear the buzz of blades, the clank of a hydraulic press, and the shouts of shearers and roustabouts against the muffled music of a radio. Lewis was contemplating the wisdom of interrupting this activity, when he heard laughter.

Walking along the road from the farmhouse were five women carrying thermoses and baskets of food. Afternoon tea. With determined swiftness, the cords to handpieces were pulled off, the last woolly rump was patted out the hatch, and all floor-sweeping stopped.

'Good afternoon, ladies,' Lewis said. 'Let me help you with those things.'

They didn't seem to mind. No-one asked who he was. The contents of the baskets were emptied onto tea-towels laid out on two bales of wool. The women teased each other as Lewis reached past them to put out mugs, a bottle of sugar, teaspoons. He helped them arrange the food, including a white platter piled high with sandwiches, and teased them back.

Some workers had slipped outside for a smoke. The old farmer, who'd been leaning on a wooden pole slicked with lanolin, was watching the women with mild amusement.

'Got yourself a new helper there, Dora?' he asked his wife.

'It's her boyfriend, Mr Davies,' a kitchen hand chirruped, causing shrieks of laughter.

'What's your name mister?' the farmer asked.

'Lewis Hammond,' he answered, accepting the cup

 Kayleen M. Hazlehurst

of tea thrust into his hand.

'And your business here?' the man persisted. 'Are you a salesman?'

Lewis flushed and looked down.

Dora touched her husband's arm. 'He's probably just seeking employment,' she said in a soft voice. The other women nodded and stared at Mr Davies as if he was being unkind.

Lewis took off his hat. 'I'm sorry, sir. I was hoping for a few days' work.'

'We only hire shearing gangs this time of year. They bring their own helpers.'

'Can you cook?' Dora asked quickly. The farmer's wife was shrewd and had seen something in Lewis.

Lewis smiled broadly. 'I do have experience in catering. I make excellent lamingtons and can knock together a fair mutton stew.'

The women turned their astonished eyes from Lewis to the boss.

The farmer nodded. 'Do you require another pair of hands in the kitchen, Dora?'

'Now, that would be very useful, Tom.'

Lewis was to present himself at the farmhouse at six the next morning. Most of his recipes he knew by heart and he wouldn't need to bring any utensils. Farmhouses were well-equipped for feeding gangs of shearers and haymakers. He was looking forward to a day in the kitchen and this set him thinking about the café. He would call the girls tomorrow, see how they were coping.

He got back to the hotel in time for dinner.

That evening he was sharing a drink with three members of The Wanton Few Motorcycle Club—Kenny, Len and Zero.

'Cool name. How'd you come up with it?' Lewis asked Kenny, the senior of the trio.

'After a local break-in a journalist wrote that it was always the wanton few who spoilt things for everyone else. We were teenagers back then and adopted the name for our own little street gang. Later we carried it over to our motorcycle club.'

'You want to see the bike I bought from Luca?'

They all knew Luca for his talent in restoring motorcycles. He could also be relied upon for finding spare parts. The four of them trailed out to inspect the Harley. Bentley watched them with narrowed eyes as they approached the truck, displaying menace by raising his upper lip to show his teeth.

'Good boy,' Lewis said, patting him through the window.

His best protection was to demonstrate he had local

     Kayleen M. Hazlehurst

connections. These men wouldn't risk Luca's ire by stealing from his most recent customer. As his new friends ran their hands admiringly over Luca's handiwork he casually mentioned he would be working for three days on the property of Dora and Tom Davies, but would be back on the weekend.

At the farmhouse the two cooks and five other ladies were kind. It was amazing how much food a shearing gang consumed in a week. Roast lamb, stewed chicken, beef casserole, shepherd's pies, pork sausages and a mountain of potatoes, along with biscuits, cakes, scones and egg-and-bacon pies for morning and afternoon teas. Lewis pitched in a sack of kūmara to the Davies household and wouldn't accept payment.

He was given a large white apron and progressively elevated from washing dishes to scrubbing root vegetables, preparing greens, and making a huge bowl of egg salad. Finally, Lewis was entrusted to make two sweets of his choosing—apple short-cake and golden sultana cake his mother had taught him from the Edmonds Cookery Book.

These were sampled by the ladies and declared to be 'quite splendid'.

Sitting on the top step of the workers' quarters, keeping

Bentley company, Lewis was enjoying a twilight beer with the shearers. It was his last evening on the farm, and the men had been okay with sharing their domain with a cook.

Jim looked up at the sky. 'Could be rain tomorrow.'

'Hope not,' said Brian, the gun shearer. 'One more day and we'll be through this mob.'

'It can rain on the weekend,' Lewis offered.

They all laughed. 'Can you cook up some fine weather for us, Lewy?'

He lifted his shoulders. 'I'll give it a go.' He tussled Bentley's head. 'Eh, boy? So, where are you blokes heading next week?'

Wayne, the contract manager, answered. 'We've got a job on the east coast. The land is steep and rough, half covered with blackberry and bracken. Better for goats, I'd say. The sheep tend to be dirty and in poor condition. We don't like shearing them but we can't turn away work.'

Brian sent Wayne a meaningful look. Wayne toyed with his car keys and looked at his nails. He'd told them earlier he was going into town. 'You want to come along as our cook, Lewis?'

'That's a mighty generous offer, but I'll be leaving on Monday. Got to get back to my own place at Limetree. I manage a little café.'

     Kayleen M. Hazlehurst

'You're a long way from home,' Jim observed. 'What brought you to the Far North?'

It was a direct question, and not altogether uncalled for. He would've been curious himself. *Should I confide in these men?*

'I have to confess, I'm looking for a little boy's pet. Wally, that's a calf, was stolen along with twenty ewes from a farm near where I live. The calf was raised thinking it was a sheep. Wally was highjacked on the same night the rustlers came. Young Sam was heartbroken.'

Wayne threw his cigarette down in disgust, but his response was cautious. 'What colour is this calf?'

'Pale gold. Jersey breed.'

'We visit a lot of farms. We'll keep our eyes open, won't we, boys?'

They all nodded and stared woefully at the horizon.

Brian shifted forward. 'Anything else you can tell us? Has this calf got any special markings or a brand? Does she wear a collar?'

'Can't say. I know she lives with sheep and might be accompanied by a scruffy black farm cat. Wally and Basil were great pals and the cat disappeared on the same night of the raid. Hopped onto the truck with the calf, we reckon.'

Wayne pulled on his wind jacket. 'Where will you be this weekend?'

'At the Waipapakauri Hotel.' Lewis stood to walk with Wayne to his car.

'I don't like your chances of recovering the stolen sheep, but someone might keep the calf as a milking cow. Do you mind if I tell your story to the boss? He's pretty fair-minded and so is the missus. The Davies family know everyone in this district. They might have a few ideas.'

Lewis extended his hand. 'I'd be grateful if you would.'

On Friday night Lewis put on his best clobber. Gail had found him a pair of black leather pants to go with her brother's leather coat. Jenny had located some fearsome looking chains, the kind bikers liked to hang about their persons. Cropped hair was acceptable and his hiking boots worked well with the rest of the gear.

He swaggered down the hotel staircase, feeling tough. No-one parted the way. They'd seen worse. At least he wasn't covered in tattoos. At the bench, Luca was the first to notice him and he signalled to the barman as Lewis approached.

'What'll it be, Lewis?'

'A lager, thanks.' He plonked himself on the next stool. A long-haired gathering wearing their patched

     Kayleen M. Hazlehurst

jackets was already at a table. Kenny raised his glass to Lewis, and the others turned their heads to take him in. Symbols and codes had real currency here and they seemed to approve. In a few minutes he would join the Wantons.

'How are ya doing, Luca?'

'Never better. Harley okay?'

'Handles well. I've given it a couple of spins on a dirt road.'

'Have you taken it on the highway?'

'Not yet. I'll be transporting it on the back of my truck but something's come up.'

'Oh, yeah?'

'I may have to carry home a calf.'

'You want me to sell you a trailer?'

'Could you fit an animal pen on the tray? Rails on three sides with a gate? It's only a small calf.'

'I guess I could weld a few railings together. When do you need it?'

'I'm leaving Monday.'

'Can you lend me your truck for the weekend?'

'I'll bring it over Saturday morning.'

The Wantons were brought up to speed but said they had no idea who was behind the sheep rustling caper. The activities of the northern gangs were no secret, Kenny explained. Even the police knew what they were up to. 'If a local gang was involved in rustling we'd have heard.'

Len agreed. 'Whoever's doing this must be acting alone.'

'Could be a single family,' Zero suggested.

Lewis decided to drop off his last sack of kūmara to the local marae before delivering his pickup to Luca. Kenny offered to follow him out to the marae. 'We should talk with the elders about the missing pet. Tell the kaumātua we want our calf back.'

'Will they know anything?' Lewis asked.

'Iwi landowners are strong, independent people. I don't think they'd pull a stunt like this. But Māori labourers get around the district and could have noticed a calf running with a bunch of sheep.'

Lewis shrugged. 'Something might turn up.'

He thought about Kenny wanting to visit the marae. It could be a friendly gesture, or to warn them something was going down. Someone had gone rogue and nobody wanted the police getting curious. There was sympathy for struggling farmers, so likely this would be discussed at the next hui.

'Hey, Kenny. Why don't you follow me out to Luca's tomorrow? We can haul off the Harley. Go for a ride.'

'Sounds good.'

 Kayleen M. Hazlehurst

On Monday, the day he was planning to leave, Lewis thought he saw an apparition. Over the weekend Bentley had been learning to ride the sidecar and they were hugging the curve of the road alongside Luca's land just before turning in. Five other motorcycles were on the driveway. Members of The Wanton Few in all their glory, looking like they were about to take a road trip.

At the centre of this assembly was Lewis' truck. He pulled up short to take in the spectacle. Luca was standing beside his handiwork, which amounted to a contraption of welded pipes with bits of metal making up a gate.

Lewis couldn't believe what was tethered inside the pen.

'What the …!'

Luca came over. 'I think this is yours.'

'Sam's calf!'

'Yep.' Kenny hopped off his bike. A girl with long black hair was sitting behind him, grinning. 'Someone delivered the calf to Luca last night.'

'Who?'

'Never seen him before,' said Luca. 'But then, I'm just an ignorant immigrant. What do I know?'

Len and Zero found this very funny. Luca had lived in this district for more than twenty years.

'Don't ask. Don't tell,' said Kenny.

Lewis held up his hands. 'Why are you all here?'

'We thought you might need help taking them back.'

'Them …?'

'Oh, didn't we say? We're waiting for someone.'

Two blasts of a horn, and a farm lorry pulled into the driveway.

'The Davies donated twenty sheep from their own flock,' Kenny said. 'Your shearer friends had something to do with that.'

'Wayne and Brian,' Lewis said. Then he noticed movement near the calf's feet. 'Crikey, Kenny. The cat!' Strapped to a rail was a cane crayfish pot and inside was a very cross Basil. Part of the pot's funnel had been trimmed away to allow the cat's spiky head to poke out. When Lewis went to examine the unique cage Basil growled, clearly unimpressed.

The boys were revving their engines.

'Are we ready to go?' Kenny was back on his bike.

'Just a minute, I have to pay for the pen.'

Luca waved his hand. 'Forget it,' he said. 'It was nothing.'

'Are you sure, mate?'

'It's my present to your little boy.'

Lewis looked around at everyone. 'Thank you for helping Sam and his family. I can't wait to see their faces.'

     Kayleen M. Hazlehurst

Kenny pointed his thumb towards his girlfriend. 'I thought you'd want to take to the road with the Wantons. Shelly, here, can drive your truck.'

⤬⤬⤬

A photograph and article appeared in the *Limetree Gazette*:

The strangest entourage arrived in town yesterday afternoon. At the lead was Lewis Hammond, Limetree's very own Antique Chef, riding a Harley-Davidson. Beside him in a side-car was his famous Labrador, Bentley, happily wearing what looked like a pair of aviator goggles!

Trailing behind Hammond were seven other vehicles. Five representatives of The Wanton Few Motorcycle Club, one pickup truck carrying a golden calf, and a lorry bearing a score of newly shorn sheep.

The meaning of this event is not yet known to the *Gazette*, but it will shortly be looked into by this newspaper ... Watch this space.

FOUR

Silver Candlesticks

THE ANTIQUE CAFÉ with its vintage clothing and nostalgic teashop had caught on in Limetree, giving the district a certain fame, if not notoriety. The cross-dressing proprietor had become a celebrity, an agony aunt of sorts for her adopted community. Not that she minded.

During the holidays visitors gravitated to the cafés, jostling with the regulars for the best tables. Louise sat with at least one person a day who needed encouragement or advice. Most problems could be sorted out over a hot drink. A mother needed help coaching a son in maths, a shy girl wanted a pretty frock for a dance, a young woman needed a stylish wedding dress in a hurry. When one lady wanted to rescue a friend from an abusive situation, Louise didn't hesitate getting Sergeant

Ronald Winfield and the Women's Shelter involved.

Her investigative skills and personal contacts were usually able to point a way forward. So, when the Anglican minister dropped in to see her she wasn't at all surprised. Gilbert Tusset was well known to her through the local choir.

'Nice to see you, Reverend. Can I offer you coffee or perhaps an early lunch?'

'Coffee, thanks. I'm only passing. Do you have time for a quick word?'

'Of course, with a slice of my pecan pie? Your favourite, if I remember.'

'Just a small piece.'

Louise ushered him to the staff table by the kitchen. 'We won't be disturbed here. Two coffees and one slice of pecan pie, please Gail.'

'You're not joining me for cake?'

She ran her hand down her snug blue and white Audrey dress. A new acquisition. 'I have to watch my figure.'

He gazed admiringly to where Gail was making their coffees and Jenny was preparing the lunch. 'It must be hard, surrounded by so much tempting food.'

Louise smiled. 'Temptation. That would be your department, Reverend. How can I help you? Does St Joseph's need some catering?'

 Kayleen M. Hazlehurst

'No, I've come here on a different matter.' The dog put his head in sympathy on the minister's knee. 'Oh, hello?'

'That's Bentley ... Nothing too serious, I hope?'

'Could be. Lately, I've noticed things disappearing from the church. This morning I was really shocked.'

'What sort of things?'

'Kneeling pillows, money from the collection plate, a whole tin of scones during the Mother's Union meeting.'

'Kids?'

'Maybe. But last night they got bolder. Two silver candlesticks were taken from the altar.'

'I see. A person could make a few bob selling those.'

'Exactly. What kind of person steals from a church? I'd prefer not to encounter someone so unfriendly when I'm alone.'

'Unfriendly, or just poor?'

'Yes. I was wondering …'

'You want me find out who's behind these thefts?'

'Honestly, I don't know where else to turn. I don't want to bother the police, especially not if it's a parishioner who's fallen on hard times.'

Louise was quiet for a moment. 'The problem is how to investigate.'

Gilbert gave a deep sigh. 'Could you hide behind a tree, or watch the building from your car?'

The minister clutched and unclutched his hands. Sunday attendance had diminished in recent years and Louise guessed church finances were getting tight. In a town like this a stakeout wouldn't go unnoticed.

'If you want me to guard the church I'll have to hide in plain sight.'

'What do you suggest?'

'Do you have an outfit for an assistant?'

Tusset's face lit up. 'You mean as a curate?'

Louise raised her eyebrows. 'Unless you'd rather I came disguised as a nun?'

The minister cast a modest glance aside. 'No, no. That wouldn't do. Certainly, I can provide the clothing. How about I put a bed for you in the vestry?'

'Now there's the idea. The thieves need to see you retire at night as normal. Can you leave out another item of value for them to steal?'

'I suppose it will be our altar cross or communion cup next. I shall be very upset if these items aren't returned to the church.'

'It's a risk, Reverend. But don't you want to get to the bottom of this?'

'Certainly. Visit me this afternoon and I'll furnish you with vestments. Will you start right away?'

'Tomorrow afternoon. Would five o'clock be all right?'

'Excellent.'

 Kayleen M. Hazlehurst

'And Reverend?'

'Yes?'

'We might need Bentley's sharp ears. Do you mind if the dog sleeps beside me in the vestry? I will bring his bed and food. We'll both be gone by morning.'

'I'll pretend I didn't hear that last question.'

At home that evening Lewis changed into his jeans and settled the blonde wig on the Styrofoam head on the dresser. After a huge bowl of assorted scraps from the café kitchen, Bentley did his usual gallop around the backyard and was nosing among the patch of silverbeet when Lewis came out to pick a few greens.

'What have you there, puppy? Have you found yourself a friend?'

Bentley nuzzled out a small black-and-white bird. A young magpie, looking frightened and very thin.

'Hello, little fella. Lost your mum?' Lewis surveyed the yard but there was no sign of a parent bird. The fledgling must have landed here after flying from a nest further away. The magpie crouched and fluttered its wings, making 'feed-me-mummy' squeaky noises.

'Ho, I see.' Lewis gathered the bird into the hammock of his hands, with Bentley jumping up to have a look.

'Down, boy. It's not a toy.'

Back in the kitchen he separated a tiny portion of the raw mince he'd planned to make into burger patties for himself and fed the fluffed-up baby worm-sized pieces. He didn't want to bring the creature into the house so he prepared a nest in a cardboard box, with a sheet of newspaper and a rag, and put it on the balcony table.

'That should do you overnight.' He wondered how long it would take a young magpie to learn to look after itself. *Two or three weeks,* he thought, as he placed a jar lid of water next to it.

It wasn't until breakfast that he noticed the magpie had a gammy leg.

Late afternoon the minister ushered his 'new curate' into the kitchen attached to the meeting room at the back of the church. He pointed to a pot on the stove. 'My wife made us supper. Vegetable soup. We can talk things over while we eat.'

'Thank you. Do you have any idea who is behind these thefts?'

'Not a one.' Tusset was a kind man, not prone to speaking ill of others.

 Kayleen M. Hazlehurst

'Have you seen anyone suspicious hanging around?'

'Only our homeless chap. Old Johnson is a war veteran and an alcoholic, but he's harmless.'

'Vietnam?'

'Yes. A tragic figure who lost his best mates during his youth. Billy Johnson would be over fifty now. Lived around here for years. The ladies of the church often make him a meal.'

'Where does he sleep?'

'On a park bench, or at the homeless refuge on the other side of town. On warm nights he favours the churchyard. He may help himself to a tin of the ladies' scones, but …'

'You doubt he'd know how to sell off a pair of silver candlesticks.'

'True. I've never known him to catch a city bus.' He wrinkled his nose. 'The driver probably wouldn't let him on board.'

'Poor guy. Then I see no reason to bother old Johnson.'

'Agreed. I've left the side door to the vestry open. There's extra clothing with a towel on your bed. I hope you'll be comfortable.'

'Very good. Bentley can stay in the truck until after dark and we'll come and go through the vestry door. We will only enter the nave if we hear noises.'

Lewis unwrapped a plate from a green tea-towel and placed it on the table.

'What have you there?'

'Leftovers from the café. Half an egg-and-bacon pie, and a couple of slices of Madeira cake.'

'They look delicious.'

'By the way, who does your book-keeping?'

'One of our members, Arnold Rodrick. He comes twice a month to do our books.'

'Have you any reason not to trust him? Does he have a drinking or gambling problem?'

'Oh no. Poor Arnold. He'd be horrified at the suggestion.' The minister stared at Lewis from under a lined brow. 'Oh dear, this pointing of fingers is very worrying.'

'Just covering all the bases. Come on, let's have a bowl of your nice soup and a piece of my cake. That will cheer us up.'

At the end of the meal the minister cleared his throat. 'My wife wanted me to ask you a question ... I apologise if it's embarrassing.'

Lewis wiped his mouth with a paper napkin. 'You can ask me anything, Gilbert.'

'Do you think you'll ever make up your mind whether you are Louise or Lewis? For us ordinary folk it can be a bit confusing. We do our best to understand ...'

 Kayleen M. Hazlehurst

'And you all do admirably. But no, I cannot say when that time will come.'

'Perhaps marriage?'

'I tried that when I was younger, but it didn't go so well.'

'No, I suppose not.' The minister gave him a resigned smile and waved his hand. 'Well, you look magnificent in your curate's outfit. Very convincing.'

Lewis passed his hands over the black cassock. 'It's surprisingly comfortable.'

'I say. Have you ever thought of joining the clergy?'

Their first night was uneventful. Lewis and Bentley patrolled the grounds twice and after a broken sleep they returned home at 6.30 am. The magpie had got out of his box and was sitting hopefully on the balcony table.

'How are we doing today, Maggie?'

Lewis checked the bird's leg. There was no sign of a break, but the left leg was definitely a centimetre shorter than the right. This injury might have been acquired in the nest or maybe it was a malformation at birth.

The magpie was noisy and grateful as he ate the minced beef. There was no reason to take him to the vet. The foot still worked, although the contracted tendon had given the bird a hobble. Sometimes Maggie preferred to stand on one leg. Either way, it explained why the fledgling had crash-landed in Lewis' backyard.

'You'll have to learn to catch your own insects,' Lewis said. 'But I guess you'll get the hang of it.'

Bentley watched on, drooling as pieces of beef were snatched up by the small beak.

Lewis put the bird back in the box and gave the dog a pat. 'Come on, boy. Time for your breakfast. You must be hungry after your job as a night watchman.'

'*Mm-m-m-m.*'

Something niggled at Louise as she dressed for the café the next morning. Her intuition urged her to wear slacks and sensible shoes that day. She couldn't get a grip on this case. No convincing profile came to mind of the person who might be conducting these thefts. *What am I missing?*

She had agreed to guard the church for a second night but doubted she would encounter a dark-cloaked figure creeping up the aisle. Before phoning all the silver bullion dealers and curio shops in the region she needed to talk again with the minister.

'Can you meet me at the café, Gilbert?'

 Kayleen M. Hazlehurst

'Is it urgent? Only I should …'

'Yes, it might be.'

'I'll come right away.'

Louise met Tusset at the front door, where Jenny was placing coffees on an outside table for customers. Bentley was already in the truck.

The minister arrived slightly out of breath. 'What's happened?'

'Nothing. But something's not right. I can feel it in my bones.'

'What is it?'

'The timing. The candlesticks themselves. I'm sorry to be so direct, but how many ladies help you at the church?'

'You mean with the dusting and cleaning?'

'And the flowers or anything else.'

'We have five regulars. They take turns.'

'We need to make certain they're all safe.'

'Heavens! Why is that?'

'I'm thinking it's possible one of those ladies took the candlesticks home to give them a polish but couldn't bring them back. Can you think who that might be?'

'Well, Mary and Helen are both married and I've heard nothing untoward about their health. Then there's Dorothy and Ruth, you know them from the choir. One has a daughter and the other lives with a son.'

'And the fifth lady?'

'Alice Blakely, also in the choir. She's sixty-three and resides on a country property out on Springfield Road. She has a big garden. Likes to do the church flowers.'

'Does Alice live alone?'

'Now you ask, I think she does.'

'When was the last time you saw her?'

'Not since the Sunday service.'

'And Monday morning you noticed the candlesticks were missing?'

'That's right ... Oh, my goodness!'

'Quickly. We can take my vehicle.'

Jenny came to the truck window. 'Is there anything I can do?'

'Call Sergeant Winfield to Alice Blakely's place on Springfield Road. Ask him to bring a couple of men. We may need a search party.'

❧

It was almost midday before the tyres of the truck turned off Springfield Road and rumbled along the gravel road towards the Blakely homestead. Alice's husband had once run a dairy farm here and now the cowshed lay in ruins. The concrete entrance had cracked from subsidence, the wooden rails were covered with moss, and the iron roof

 Kayleen M. Hazlehurst

had fallen in. On the nine kilometre drive out of town, Louise learned that there were no children to inherit this property. It would go the way of too many small farms and probably be turned into subdivisions for housing.

As they approached the farmhouse the yard was strangely quiet, apart from a few foraging hens. No household animals came out to greet them.

'Where are her pets?' Gilbert asked. 'Alice dotes on that dog of hers, and her cat is usually sunning itself on the doorstep.'

'What's the dog called?'

'Lucy, maybe ... No Sadie. From the song *Sadie the Cleaning Lady.* That's how I remember it. She's a long-haired border collie. Lovely natured.'

'Maybe the pets are inside.' Louise yanked on the brake and was already striding towards the front door as the minister climbed from the truck with Bentley. 'Could you search the garden while I go through the house?' she called back. 'Bentley will help you. Sergeant Winfield should be here any minute.'

Louise didn't know what she would find. The absence of relaxed and happy pets in the forecourt heightened her suspicion that their mistress had been unable to feed them. Alice Blakely was in trouble, she was sure of it.

A brief knock brought no answer, so she let herself in by the unlocked front door. In the hallway she started to call Alice's name, passing by the tidy kitchen and into a comfortable living room that faced the back garden. Through the window she saw Bentley and Gilbert fossicking between rows of petunias and flowering shrubs. To his credit, this nervous man was scouring every corner of the garden looking for clues of his lost parishioner.

Louise was now running. Up the staircase and onto the landing, checking all three bedrooms, the bathroom, the sewing room, the loft. The upper level of the house showed no derangement. Alice's handbag was on the bed and there'd been no apparent burglary. No signs of human collapse from a heart attack or stroke. No evidence of a distressed lady of any sort or of her beloved pets—either fed or starving.

The front door banged shut behind her.

'She's not inside,' Louise shouted as the minister emerged from the tool shed. 'Did you find anything?'

'Nothing. I was about to check the garage if you'd like to join me.'

They walked together towards the single garage that stood to the left of the driveway and began to raise the door when they heard a siren. Two police cars came steaming down the road towards them.

'I'll finish the garage while you talk with the police,'

    Kayleen M. Hazlehurst

Tusset said. He sounded confident now, as if he was on top of this detection business.

Louise had barely finished explaining the situation to Sergeant Winfield and his off-siders, Neville and Lance, when the minister burst from the garage waving the candlesticks and a bottle of Silvo Polish.

'You were spot on, Louise! Alice *had* brought the candlesticks home. I've just found these in her car.'

The sergeant looked irritated. 'So, where is she? Could she have gone away?'

'Not without her handbag or telling her friends,' Louise pointed out.

'And not without returning church property,' asserted the minister.

'Gilbert's right.' Louise sighed. 'The candlesticks are our best evidence that Alice is still here. I'll bet she's had a fall and her pets are with her somewhere.'

Tusset shoved a woollen garment at Louise. 'I found her cardigan in the car. Isn't your Bentley a search and rescue hound?'

Winfield laughed. 'Let's hope he remembers his training.'

'Have a little faith, Ronald.' Louise clicked on the dog leash. 'How do you want to play this?'

'You take Bentley. The rest of us can fan out over the field.' He turned to his constables. 'Separate as far as you can without losing sight of each other. We must cover every inch of these paddocks.'

'Righto, Sarge.'

He turned back to Louise. 'If you're so certain Alice is here then I'd better radio for an ambulance.'

'Yes, let's be positive. The poor woman's been missing for three days.'

'Crikey!' The sergeant was really an old softie in a crisis.

'The last time she was seen was Sunday morning.'

'Okay, boys. No mucking about. Imagine you're looking for your dear old granny. No stone unturned.'

The policemen strode off towards the paddocks with Tusset keenly joining their line.

Louise had a different plan. She bent to offer Bentley the cardigan. 'Here, get a sniff of this. That's it, good boy. Find the trail for us.'

'*Mm-m-m-m.*'

⚜

The men were well into the first paddock by the time Bentley latched onto a scent. He pawed at the wooden side gate behind the tool shed. The garden paths were spread with pebbles and shells but past the gate this changed into flattened grass. A trail used occasionally,

   Kayleen M. Hazlehurst

Louise assumed, by an elderly lady who knew it well. When she opened the gate Bentley almost tore the leash from her hand.

They hadn't gone far when the contour of the field dipped away and the ground became pitted with hoof prints and hardened tufts of grass. Ahead, the hill curved down to a damp gully populated by weeping willows. Before Bentley's strong shoulders pulled her out of sight Louise was able to catch Gilbert's attention, hoping her waving arm communicated that the search team should come her direction.

As she suspected, the gully discharged a spring. This produced a marshy area that was ideal for a good harvest of white arum lilies. Lily groves like this were planted on many early New Zealand farms when these flowers were believed to have a certain enigmatic charm. White lilies, a symbol of purity and rebirth in Victorian times, continued to be chosen as sympathy flowers. An older woman might require them for the funerals of friends or to decorate a church.

As Louise approached she called out Alice's name. Bentley stood stock-still to listen but Louise could only hear the distant howl of a farm dog.

Bentley knew otherwise. He raised his nose to the sky in a wail, then he snapped the leash from her hand and lurched down the hill.

'They're here! They're here!' Louise screamed as the men appeared above the rim of the hill.

The five of them, slipping and sliding, followed Bentley to where they could see the crumpled heap of a human figure. Partially covering her mistress was the shaggy body of Sadie, her long tail wagging with delight that help had finally arrived.

'Alice! Alice! Can you hear me?' Louise could see the sharp end of a bone protruding through a torn stocking. Spread across the ground was an armful of fallen flowers. 'Don't worry dear, we're here. We'll take care of you.'

Winfield knelt to gently lift away the reluctant pet. 'There girl. We'll look after her now. Good dog.'

Roused to consciousness, Alice was able to explain she had slipped and broken her ankle walking home after gathering lilies from the gully. She had lain on the hillside for two days and two nights, with only her raincoat and Sadie's warmth to protect her.

The sergeant swung into action. His two constables were told to return to the house. 'Neville, bring back our blanket and first aid kit from the car. Lance, you wait for the ambulance men. Show them where to come.'

Alice was stretchered out of the paddock, along with a shaking Sadie in Winfield's arms. As they trudged up the grassy hill a black-and-white cat, her tail crooked in a question mark, appeared from nowhere—zigging and

 Kayleen M. Hazlehurst

zagging, mewing and crying, running ahead and then waiting for her mum to be carried home.

❦

The *Limetree Gazette* gave the local police a glowing write-up of the 'miraculous rescue', with a photograph of Sergeant Winfield handing back the silver candlesticks to Reverend Tusset on the steps of St Joseph's Church.

The occupants of the Blakely residence were invited to move in with Louise. She could hardly leave anyone behind while Alice recuperated. Chez Louise's was now a menagerie of two people, two dogs, one cat and a magpie, with the chooks being fostered out to a friend.

Bentley took it all in his stride and the cat claimed the warmest spot on the back porch. The widow was an appreciative guest. She knitted each dog a jacket for the coming winter and Louise was tactfully knitted a scarf.

Alice said she didn't mind what clothes Louise wore, or whether she was Louise or Lewis. She was only waiting for the day when she could stand without crutches to do some of her favourite baking for the café.

FIVE

The Prodigal Son

THEY WERE SITTING after dinner on the back porch as the setting sun echoed across a low blanket of cloud, tinging with pink the weatherboards and cream bricks of the houses. Bentley and Sadie lay at their feet, having licked their bowls clean. Cleo was curled by the living room fire and the adopted magpie had joined them on the outside table, hopping as usual on his best leg.

Alice glanced with concern at Louise. 'This would be Sergeant Winfield's idea, I presume. It's not as if you're on the police payroll. Don't you realise how dangerous this proposal is?'

The widow had settled happily into Shepherds Lane as Louise's guest, but she felt the local constabulary took advantage of her friend's willingness to help people in trouble.

'I have no qualifications as a detective, so my work has to be off the books. Anyway, the family are offering to cover my expenses.'

'Well, it's a funny old business if you ask me. Why must it be you?'

Louise shrugged. 'Perhaps they think I have some special entrée into that world.'

'The red-light district, you mean. You'll be eaten alive by those people.'

'It's only a missing person. I don't intend to stay long.' She reached to pat Alice's forearm. 'I'm not a babe in the woods, you know.'

'You are to me, dear. And this time they want you to go to Australia.'

'Ah, about that. Do you mind looking after the animals?'

The Australian authorities had no interest in locating a lost boy whose last known address was Kings Cross.

'They say they have enough to do without chasing runaway Kiwis,' Sergeant Winfield related to Lewis when he dropped in at the station. 'We need someone who's capable of making a few enquiries ... Look the lad in the eye and tell him all is forgiven.'

     Kayleen M. Hazlehurst

'And you think that capable person is me?'

The sergeant adjusted his shoulders. 'You know your way around these ...'

'... kinds of places?'

'... big cities.'

'I worked in the finance sector in Auckland, Ronald. I wasn't a transvestite.'

'I know ... Sorry ... Not suggesting ...' He waved his arm at the young constables behind their desks. 'You have a whole lot more experience of city life than my country coppers. Wet behind the ears, most of them. If anyone can find Jason without a fuss, it's you.'

'You mean I'll know how to blend in.'

'Something like that. How about I take you to meet the Millers? Nice folks. See how you feel once you've had a chat.'

'Was there a family tiff of some kind?'

'Don't know. You'll have to ask.'

Lewis doubted the young man was in any real danger, he'd probably just found employment or moved on. But the parents were worried. The mere mention of Kings Cross had set off alarm bells.

At Kingsford Smith Arrivals Lewis was met by a

uniformed member of the NSW Police, holding up a sign.

'Hello. Are you looking for me? I'm Lewis Hammond.'

'Gidday, Lewis. Glad to meet you. Senior Constable Aaron Reilly.' The policeman extended his hand. 'I hear you know my old mate, Ronald Winfield.'

Lewis smiled. 'Ronny and I are in the same choir.'

'The same choir, eh? That's a new one. Welcome to Sydney. I'm told you're here to find a missing teenager.'

'Yes, Jason Miller.'

'How old is this kid?'

'Almost twenty. His father is unwell and his mother is frantic for him to come home and help with their carpet business.'

'Like me to show you around tomorrow?'

'No thanks. I have a map.'

Reilly handed over a card. 'Here's my phone number. You can find me at Kings Cross Police Station. Righto. Let's get you to your hotel.'

The Sebel, a European-styled establishment in Elizabeth Bay, had seen better days. It was once a hangout for musicians and performers. Elton John had stayed there when he got married. By the 1980s the district around Kings Cross and Darlinghurst had gained a sleazy reputation. Adult entertainment and dimly lit nightclubs

 Kayleen M. Hazlehurst

drew in throngs of customers to the tourist hotels in the area.

When Lewis opened the door to Room 204 he was confronted by a stained carpet, faded curtains and the lingering odour of stale tobacco. Needless to say, Senior Constable Reilly had deposited him in exactly the right place for his investigations. Public transport gave him easy access to the areas between Potts Point and Paddington.

He put his suitcase on the solitary chair and stared out at the leafy street, then ran a finger along the window sill. It had been a while since it was graced by a duster. After a meal and a shower, he'd fallen into a moderately comfortable bed and slept the whole night.

He woke to a quiet knock and the sound of a key slipping into a lock. Across the hall a woman's voice was calling, 'Housekeeping.'

Lewis spoke through the slightly ajar door. 'Maybe tomorrow, thanks.'

He checked his watch. He'd missed the hotel breakfast but there would be plenty of cafés. After changing into his best shirt and jeans, he slipped on a pair of leather loafers. Today there'd be lots of walking.

The Black Bean, a street vender offering coffee and egg-and-bacon sandwiches, sorted him out for breakfast. The Salvation Army Outreach Centre on Victoria

Street would be his first place of enquiry.

Coming over to Australia on Air New Zealand Lewis had asked himself where a young man with little money could go for help. The Salvation Army was known to offer hot drinks and possibly some advice about how to get started in a big city. If the Salvos were really a mecca for young runaways, there might have been a temporary bed there for Jason.

As Lewis neared the centre of Kings Cross he looked up and saw a huge Coca-Cola sign. It stood out like a beacon on the city horizon, beckoning punters to places that were more notorious.

Through a glass partition a matronly woman checked a register.

Captain Davies turned to the 1993 entries. 'Which month was it?'

'May or June.'

'Ah, yes. Jason Miller. He stayed at the men's shelter for three nights. I'm sorry, there's no forwarding address.' The woman smiled kindly. 'A well-mannered young man, as I recall.'

'Glad to hear it. His parents are lovely.'

A man introducing himself as Major Stanford joined them. 'Sydney is a magnet for disaffected youth,' he explained.

 Kayleen M. Hazlehurst

Captain Davies gave a sad nod. 'It breaks my heart to see so many young ones living on the streets. We wish they all had caring families like your lovely Millers.'

'Have you considered the hospitals?' the Major asked.

'Not yet.'

'Oh, but you must. The lad might have met with an accident. St Vincent's is our nearest emergency department.'

The officers hovered while Lewis dialled a number pinned to a wall and looked relieved when no record of a patient named Jason Miller was found. After thanking Lewis for his visit, they saw him to the door and wished him every success in his search for the prodigal son.

Later Lewis stopped in at the Wayside Chapel on Hughes Street. Major Stanford had mentioned Reverend Ted Noffs and his drop-in centre for the destitute—away from the bawdy saloons with their long tentacles of alcohol and drugs.

Lewis didn't know what he would find at the Wayside, other than a cheap coffee and a leaflet warning about the lifestyles that were trapping youngsters. Alcohol was one thing, but the culture of drugs and prostitution involved criminal elements that were predatory and ruthless. If Jason was caught up in this scene Lewis urgently wanted to let him know that help was here.

The Wayside had no information, but it was suggested Lewis join their workers on street surveillance the following evening. Alan and Stan took their usual route in their old white van with the words WAYSIDE CHAPEL painted in blue on the side. They drove slowly, pulling up to speak with shivering prostitutes, and to make sure fallen drunks didn't need medical attention or collapsed addicts weren't in a coma. What hadn't he noticed, he wondered, on those nights he'd left his Auckland office and driven home to his unhappy wife in the warm suburbs?

Alan pulled in beside a park sidewalk where rough sleepers emerged from the shrubbery to receive a tub of hot food or a packet of sandwiches. Hot drinks were prepared in the back of the van by a volunteer named Sophie. These angels of the street were known and trusted, Lewis realised. He searched every profile beneath the woollen hats and hoods—quietly comparing them to the school photograph in his shirt pocket, listening for any signs of a Kiwi accent. There were few opportunities to mention Jason's name without causing suspicion. A cordon of silence separated the street people from the police, but not from those who might prey on them.

At the end of the vigil they dropped him off at the Sebel.

     Kayleen M. Hazlehurst

'You might have to widen your search to the pubs and clubs,' Alan said.

'Anything I should look out for?'

Stan jerked back his head. 'Watch out for wandering hands.'

'Good tip.'

Alan gave his colleague a playful punch. 'Shut up Stan. We'll keep our ears open Lewis, though don't be too hopeful. People often change their names or invent street ones.'

'So they can't be found,' clarified Stan.

'I'll do some scouting around. Thanks for the evening. Can't say I enjoyed it, but the company was good.' He grinned. 'A real eye-opener.'

They waved him goodbye at the hotel doorstep and roared off. 'Don't be a stranger!' Sophie yelled through the window.

He hadn't really expected the Salvos or Wayside to throw up any clues, but he *had* been hopeful.

⚜

The plan the next evening was to explore the pub-rock scene. Louise was taking public transportation to spare herself blisters from walking in high heels. She wanted to visit the famous Sandringham Hotel near Newtown

Station, and any other pubs along the way that might provide employment for young Kiwis.

As she walked down King Street—past the old bookshops, second-hand clothes stores, night markets and the hole-in-the-wall eateries serving carafes of cheap wine—she could see the spaces where Sydney's alternative cultures thrived. Strains of pop, rock, punk, blues and even folk music seeped out onto the streets. Clusters of Goths and Punks exhibiting pink and green hair and strange outfits were bubbling along with the other cliques and tribes towards their favourite night haunts.

At the 'Sando' she found a place to perch at one of the circular tables. A live band was belting out a Jimmy Barnes song near a bar counter laid out in a square, which allowed musicians to order beers between gigs. It was early, and the dance floor beside the stage was still empty. Heavy drinkers preferred to stand, and the waiters carried trays of drinks to the scattered tables.

'What will it be, lady?' she was asked.

'A shandy, thanks.'

Louise studied the serving staff. None of them looked familiar. While the crowd revelled in the music she caught hostile stares from two men propped up at the bar. Their lips curled down as they drew in close to talk. Soon she would have to leave. Both hotel toilets would be unavailable to her dressed in a frock, and the insults

     Kayleen M. Hazlehurst

would start to come with the drunkenness. After an hour she decided she'd be safer at a gay bar.

Gay bashings on Oxford Street had made news across the Tasman. She'd heard police weren't terribly interested in making arrests for these violent crimes. Despite this, a relaxation of homosexual laws had brought greater public acceptance and same-sex couples were making their homes in the terraces and apartments of Darlinghurst and Paddington.

As the bus let off passengers at Oxford Street, other figures stepped from the overhang of an empty shop to climb on board. Something on the edge of her vision made her nerves tingle. A certain energy, or maybe it was pure instinct. As she turned down the street she felt a flicker of disturbance in the atmosphere.

Louise quickened her step but didn't run. She wouldn't give the buggers the satisfaction. The footsteps were soft at first, as if they were closing ground on the trotting pads of wolves, then they became heavy with intent. One hand grasped her shoulder and another was reaching for her backside. She seized the approaching hand and spun around, twisting it behind the assailant's back.

Her voice dropped an octave. 'Keep your paws to yourself, mate. Unless you want me to break your arm.'

The man's face was a picture of surprise and stupefaction, but Louise's advantage didn't last for long. A blow between her shoulder blades from an accomplice sent her flying. The ugly profanity shocked her, even before she hit the pavement. There were sneering taunts as her wig fell away and the sound of fabric tearing when the boots went in.

The shriek of a whistle was followed by shouting and an eruption of running feet. Someone was kneeling beside her, pulling her hands away from her head. Speaking gently.

He had a kind face and was wearing a red beret and bomber jacket. 'Don't be afraid. We're here now. Those punks who attacked you have taken off.'

A voice answered. Her own. Except it was as though she was speaking down a wind tunnel. 'Who … who are you?'

'We're the Guardians. We work this patch.'

Several young faces with berets were peering over the shoulder of the guy in charge. For a moment Louise thought she'd stepped into someone's film shoot.

She sat up, rubbing the lump on her forehead. 'Who did you say you were?'

     Kayleen M. Hazlehurst

Her rescuer pointed at the symbol on his white T-shirt—a triangle with an eye, and two wings. 'We're the Guardian Angels,' he repeated. 'People call us vigilantes, but we're really just a safety patrol. We watch the streets and public transport. Make sure there's no trouble.'

'You stopped the fighting?'

'We stopped the thrashing, mate. Three of them were about to do you over. You're lucky we arrived when we did. People have been killed.'

More bystanders were gathering. They were rubber-necking down the street and a few were muttering about going after the culprits.

'Who are all these people?'

'They've come out from The Midnight Shift.' He pointed to a pub down the street. 'The customers are angry there's been another incident.'

Louise touched her ribs and winced. 'Sorry, I'm a bit dazed ...'

'Here, let's get you on your feet.' The patrol leader brushed her down and gallantly handed back her wig. 'Want us to take you to hospital?'

'No thanks, I'm a bit bruised, that's all. Is there somewhere I can sit down?'

'We'll go into the pub. I know the girls. They'll look after you.' He smiled. 'My name's Tony, by the way. What's yours?'

She shoved on her wig, wishing she had a mirror to make sure she didn't look a fright. 'I'm Louise. Do you always work nights?'

'Yeah, mostly. We move around a bit. Now you see us, now you don't.'

'The Guardian Angels, eh? Never heard of you. Hell, I wouldn't care if you were called the Purple Knights of the Jedi Starfighters. You're all heroes to me.'

Tony laughed. 'Come on. The Golden Girls are performing tonight. I'll introduce you.'

The Golden Girls were finishing their eyelashes and adjusting their frou-frou skirts. Tony seemed comfortable enough to take Louise backstage, where he offered her a chair and fetched a warm drink. He spoke to one of the girls in the dressing room. Then with a cheery smile and a backward wave, he rushed away.

Louise sipped her tea as three of the girls came over to inspect the damage. They stroked her face and patted her shoulder.

'Hello, I'm Annabelle. Will you be okay while we do our show?'

'If you don't mind me sitting here for a few minutes?'

'Of course you can. Poor lamb.'

'I'm Zara. You look terrible. Vicky, get Louise a couple of biscuits before she faints.'

 Kayleen M. Hazlehurst

Vicky handed Louise two chocolate biscuits on a plate. 'Here you go. Choccy bikkies always help.'

'Corker, thanks.'

'You can watch us from the wings,' Zara added.

Annabelle led the entourage onto the stage with the panache of a star in her diamante jewellery, Marilyn Monroe wig, and white satin evening gown split to the thigh. She had the figure and slinky stride of a youth, with the knowingness of a veteran in her mid-thirties. Vicky, Zara, Poppy and Vanessa tottered after her to perform as backup singers to the premixed music, which the girls mimed flawlessly. The audience sang along, amidst the lights and glitz, and puffs of dry ice, clapping ferociously at the end.

Louise had never warmed to the drag-queen scene in Auckland and was reminded why she had turned her back on all this and opted for a quiet life in the country. Big cities might seem exotic but, in the dark shadows and under the fluorescent lights, the truth was not so grand. Alone in the wings with her battered misery she was feeling strangely homesick. She was just a little cross-dresser who was as happy to be Louise as she was to be Lewis. Her friends at Limetree had grown to accept her for this as well.

After the show the Golden Girls tidied up her gashed face, applied their own special salve of witty banter and glass of bubbly, then ordered a taxi to take Louise back to the hotel. As she limped from the bar she looked over the sea of festive figures and wondered how on earth she would ever find Jason Miller.

❧

Lewis stared up as the morning light crept over the hotel ceiling, speculating on what could have happened to a country boy after he moved to the big smoke. He could have done without the beating yesterday but was glad to have met the Guardian Angels, particularly Tony. *What a cool guy. Will I ever see him again?* It made him realise how much he admired brave, compassionate men. Even brave, compassionate dogs like Bentley. It was a role model absent in his life when he was growing up. *Give me a break. I was only two when my father abandoned us.*

As a boy he felt confused about who he was. Who he should become. Even when he got married he hadn't quite grown into his own skin. But he knew what he *didn't* admire—the thugs and con-men, the rapacious bully-boys of the streets and boardroom. Knowing what you weren't was a good place to start. Sometimes you had to work backwards when you were trying to figure things out. Yet his own tangled truth still seemed caught up in a web of separation and loss.

 Kayleen M. Hazlehurst

All this introspection had awakened some latent strengths. His powers of observation and analysis. When Sergeant Winfield took him to meet Jason's parents they were reluctant to reveal any family secrets—information that could have been useful. They only admitted that their son had followed a school mate to Sydney. The Millers didn't express their disapproval directly, but it was clear they believed Jason had fallen under bad influences.

There had to be more to the story? Why did the parents assume the two friends had been seduced by the Bohemian lifestyle of Kings Cross? Wouldn't they prefer to find work and start their adult lives like other young people?

What the Millers didn't say spoke volumes. Campaigns for Gay Rights had generated a sense of liberation in the gay community, and a certain euphoric drift into the Sydney inner suburbs. Were one or both of these young men gay? Had there been some altercation between father and son? A threat of disownment? A rejection of parental authority? Were there hurt feelings that needed to be appeased, or broken fences that couldn't be mended?

What exactly had pushed Jason Miller away from Limetree and propelled him so suddenly to Sydney?

Lewis was coming to understand the ethos around him. Mental maps were forming. A sense of how each street was tuned to the whole urban orchestra. The cultures and codes of the street-wise. Yet, in three weeks he'd found no trace of the lost son.

The senior constable at Kings Cross Police Station was sympathetic. 'Missing persons are tough cases,' Aaron Reilly said. 'Especially if people don't want to be found. No-one would blame you if you gave up, Lewis.'

'I'm not there yet. There's another week on my air ticket.'

'Good on you, mate. If there's anything the police can do ...'

'Thanks. Most of it is legwork, unless you think I've missed something?'

'Have you considered the morgue?'

Lewis swallowed hard. 'The morgue?'

'Don't you follow the news? A lot of those folks you've been chasing are dying from AIDS.'

'Those folks, being?'

'Poofters, mate. I'm surprised you haven't thought of it.'

Lewis clenched his fists. Not because he wanted to clout the idiot, but to take back his self-control. Yes, he'd heard about the epidemic among the gay population, but the idea that Jason might be dead hit him hard.

'Good suggestion,' Lewis said briskly, then he turned and strode from the station.

 Kayleen M. Hazlehurst

St Vincent's private and public hospitals in Darlinghurst shared the same mortuary. There would be records of deceased patients who had never been claimed.

In the foyer Lewis was surprised to see the head of St Vincent's AIDS clinic, Professor Ron Penny, had been granted a Queen's Birthday Honour in June. A photograph of Professor Penny, along with a recent newspaper article, was pinned on a display board. The esteemed immunologist and his team were working at speed to test new antiviral drugs.

Lewis had already seen the fear of the 'gay plague' in Auckland. As the world mocked and blamed, certain hospitals and government departments in the Antipodes had set up public education campaigns. By the early nineties messages discouraging 'unsafe sex' and the 'sharing of needles' were beginning to gain traction in the community.

Here in Sydney, hospitals like St Vincent's were experimenting with AIDS treatments, a spokesman explained. Medical staff were determined to provide pain relief to suffering patients and to suppress acquired infections. The article emphasised this was not only a homosexual disease. It could be transmitted to anyone through the exchange of bodily fluids, including blood.

That's right, blood transfusions, thought Lewis. *These happen after car accidents or during surgeries.*

At the reception desk Lewis dithered. There was still no record of a Jason Miller being admitted into the hospital. 'Would you mind checking the morgue?' he asked shyly.

The receptionist pursed her lips, then obligingly scanned through her computer. 'He's certainly not in the morgue. Is there anything else we can help you with? You seem worried.'

Until now Lewis had never thought to ask about Jason's friend. *What was his name? Leo somebody.* He searched his memory. 'Do you have anyone by the name of Leo Daniels?'

The receptionist glanced around. 'I'm not supposed to give information unless you are family.'

'I've been appointed by the Miller family to find Jason and that includes me checking the hospitals. He may have been accompanied by a friend. It would help a lot if I could cross them both off my list.'

'Get yourself a coffee while I check the records,' she whispered.

As he walked towards the hospital café he was conscious that behind these walls were beds filled with the sick and dying. Young lives wasting away. Men, and a

     Kayleen M. Hazlehurst

few women, vulnerable to every form of human infection. AIDS was a death sentence for all of them.

When Lewis came back the receptionist was standing outside her cubicle with a colleague. She nodded at him as he approached.

'This man is from New Zealand,' she told the nurse. 'He's been sent here by the family to find their son.' She handed over a file. 'Please take him to the AIDS ward.'

Lewis felt blood drain from his face.

'This way please,' the nurse said as she briskly led him away. At the entrance to Ward 17 South she put on protective clothing and handed Lewis a mask. 'This is optional,' she said. 'It's quite safe to talk.'

The first thing that struck him when the doors swung open was the emaciated figures. Some three dozen male patients, in bays of six beds, were withering away from rare diseases and organ failure. The stench of soiled sheets and disinfectant assailed his senses. Horror might have impaled him but, instead, he was overcome by something entirely different.

Despite the cries of anguish, the ward was being run with efficiency and compassion. Male and female nurses were touching their patients, turning them tenderly and feeding those who could take sustenance. At adjoining bedsides, he saw a priest and a rabbi. Visitors were staying to help. They were holding loved ones' hands and eating lunch with them.

In a corner a fair-headed man embraced a sick friend. 'This is Leo Daniels,' the nurse said, stopping at the foot of the bed. 'Have a nice visit.'

The moment the visitor turned, Lewis recognised his face from the photo he carried in his shirt pocket. Jason Miller, who looked to be in the peak of good health, had been caring for his old school friend all this time.

Alice put down a mug of hot coffee, accompanied by two slices of toast. In an hour Louise would have to leave for work and Gail and Jenny would have already opened Louise's Vintage Café.

'You look sad, dear,' Alice said.

'Yes. It was a sad journey.'

'A sad city by the sounds of it. Will it change for the better, do you think?'

'I'm sure it will. I saw amazing things happening in the short time I was there.'

Alice gave a deep nod. 'Tell me the whole story. How did those poor boys get themselves into such a pickle?'

'After high school Leo got the bright idea of finding

 Kayleen M. Hazlehurst

work in Sydney. They agreed to meet up in a couple of months once Leo found his feet.'

'I expect they were both excited. So, what went wrong?'

'Leo stayed in a cheap motel until his money ran out. With no work, he ended up sleeping rough.'

'Oh, dear. Things can be so difficult without family.'

'Every day was a struggle. The church groups gave him some help but …'

'It wasn't enough.'

'No. Life on the streets was precarious. He had to sleep in the bushes to avoid the street gangs. Eventually he was taken in by a man who ran some kind of flop-house and this Fagin character coaxed him into becoming a sex worker.'

'Poor lad.'

'He couldn't earn enough money to get away and soon discovered that heroin took away the pain. He had to continue the sex work in order to support his habit.'

'All those awful people pushing drugs onto our young people. You'd think the police would do more to protect them.'

'That wasn't the worst of it. Leo contracted HIV, either from the sex work or from sharing needles. The Wayside workers found him crumpled in a heap from an overdose.'

'Did they take him straight to hospital?'

'Leo only remembers being sick and terrified. He was so broken they put him into the psych ward at St Vincent's.'

'That's when he sent a message to Jason to come quickly?'

Louise nodded. 'Not long after they transferred Leo to the AIDS ward.'

Alice clasped her hands around her coffee mug and sighed. 'I can see it all now. Jason rushed to Leo's side after having a major quarrel with his parents.'

'So it seems. Every day Jason came to the hospital to be with Leo. He felt desperately sorry for the patients and inspired by the staff who were trying to save their lives.'

'The nurses were run off their feet, so Jason started to help?' Alice queried.

'Yes. First it was mopping up messes, then it was delivering food or linen. Beds in the ward had to be changed several times a day. Naturally, the nurses put in a good word and he was offered free food and a small wage for his labours. Because he was willing to work any shift, the hospital provided him with a tiny room and a bed. Little more than a glorified cupboard, but he was grateful for the accommodation.'

'That boy's life revolved around the hospital from the minute he arrived in Sydney.'

 Kayleen M. Hazlehurst

'Pretty much.'

'I'm not surprised you couldn't find him, Louise.'

'When I finally visited the hospital, I found a committed young man who was loved by everyone. Jason liked to crack jokes and even Leo was a funny guy.'

'That's nice. Will Leo live, do you suppose?'

'We can only hope there'll be some kind of medical breakthrough.'

'I'll ask the minister to pray for them next Sunday.'

'Thanks, Alice. But Jason won't be coming home for a while. I'll have to break the news to his parents.'

'Let me come with you, dear. We'll persuade the Millers this is a good outcome. Jason is in excellent health and he has taken an interest in worthwhile work.'

'It's true. He wants to become a male nurse and the hospital administration is helping him apply for training.'

'Sounds like he has the perfect temperament.'

She laughed. 'The nursing staff called him Florence. They were always teasing him.'

'As in Nightingale, I presume. His parents should be proud.'

'I'm not sure they will be, given …'

'Well, we shall have to convince them. We will help the Millers understand how fortunate they are to have such a caring son.'

'You're a bloody marvel, old girl.'

'Don't be daft!' Alice swept off cackling to fetch them a second mug of coffee.

Settled again in Limetree—with its green rolling farmland, its odd country folk, and its ageing houses and shops—Louise felt a genuine sense of homecoming. She was not going back to Australia, no matter how much Ronald Winfield begged.

In the backyard the dogs were playing rough-and-tumble on the dewy grass, the cat was stalking through the spinach patch looking for lizards, and a congregation of magpies were warbling their hearts out on the wooden fence.

At this moment Louise's only companion was their little rescue-bird. Maggie was hopping towards his breakfast set out on the outside table. Three other magpies began edging along the fence, their eyes fixed on the minced beef. The birds had adopted the right posture for success, each hopping on one leg.

 Kayleen M. Hazlehurst

SIX

Alpacas! Alpacas!

LEWIS LEANED ON the wooden railing overlooking a paddock. Twenty adult birds plus four hundred chicks at varying stages of maturity were pecking over the pasture. A friend had asked for advice about an investment opportunity. Todd Finch, a thirtyish schoolteacher who was presently courting a farmer's daughter, had been buttonholed by a stranger in a pub with a tempting proposition. Lewis had asked for a couple of days to investigate.

Exotic animals were not easy farming enterprises. Unlike the goat craze of the mid-1980s, the importation of camelids from Chile—alpacas and llamas—had been expensive and controversial, involving lengthy quarantine periods. Sheep and cattle were New Zealand's gold and oil and nobody wanted foot-and-mouth disease to enter the country. Even more worrying was the recent love affair with Australian emus. With all their voluptuous beauty and feathered tails, gullible investors were being drawn into schemes that appeared to benefit only a few experienced players. There had been talk of controlling parties in India and whispers of fraud in the press.

'We should visit this emu farm,' Lewis suggested when Todd first raised the question. 'Make sure this offer is genuine.'

'The farm is open to the public on weekends. Would Sunday be all right for you? It's a three-hour drive.'

'Sunday's fine.'

Todd outlined the project as they drove to a rural district south-west of Hamilton. Pioneering farmers who'd purchased mated pairs of the birds were supposedly reaping big rewards. Emu eggs and chicks could be bought and sold-on to future investors.

'It's a sure thing,' Todd enthused. 'You can triple your money.'

What could Lewis say in the face of such eagerness? Of the countries he'd researched there didn't seem to be much of a market for emu by-products. In Japan a few restaurants had entered into a mild flirtation with the lean red meat, but the response of consumers was lukewarm. Americans preferred a nicely marbled beef steak and

     Kayleen M. Hazlehurst

people in the Antipodes loved their roast lamb. Even in India emu fat was not widely used as a cooking oil and in Australia emu leather hadn't taken off as predicted. Although at airports Lewis had noticed new lines of 'pure Australian emu oil' for inflammatory joint and skin conditions competing for the tourist dollar.

Lewis waved his hand over the paddock they had come to examine.

'What happens to all these chicks?

'The emu farmer looks after the breeding pairs and their offspring. He does all the selling of chicks on behalf of investors.'

'I see. So you're not bringing your birds back to Limetree?'

'No, they stay here. Buyers pay for their upkeep—a bit for food and a contribution towards fencing. It's cheaper that way. I don't have to buy a piece of land or anything.'

'So the deal is only on paper. You simply hand over your dosh?'

Todd hesitated. 'I suppose …'

'What is this emu farmer trying to sell you?'

'A fertilised egg costs about sixty dollars. A one-day old chick is a hundred dollars and a three-month-old chick is three hundred. It's very cheap. In America and Britain people are paying thousands.'

'And the price of a breeding pair?'

'Five thousand dollars, but you can make a packet selling their chicks.'

During his years as a financial adviser Lewis had noticed how greed could drive investors into a buying frenzy. Claims of inflated profits always aroused his suspicions. Before him he could see actual birds on an actual property, but to him the venture had the stench of a pyramid scheme. Down the track he foresaw squandered life-savings and civil lawsuits.

'They're interesting birds, Todd. But what's to stop this farmer from selling your eggs and emus to more than one buyer? None of the birds appear to be tagged.'

'I'm sure it's legit. I've seen photos ...'

'What if the bottom falls out of the market? What if you are the buyer at the end of the queue? This emu farmer could pack up one dark night and disappear to Bali with the money he took from you and hundreds of other investors.'

Todd looked down at his muddy boots. 'I never thought about that.'

'I suggest you take a deep breath before you throw your hard-earned cash in this direction. I don't want to see you lose the shirt off your back.'

Todd's face crumpled with disappointment, but he wanted one last chance to stand up for himself. 'What

 Kayleen M. Hazlehurst

makes you so sure?' he said defensively. 'People are saying it's foolproof!'

'Ah, mate. It isn't foolproof. It's almost certainly a scam.'

'But it seems so ...'

'So real? I know.' Lewis put a hand on Todd's shoulder. 'Come on. We'll get some fish and chips and I'll explain to you the pitfalls of circular trading and pyramid schemes on the way home.'

Todd dropped Lewis off at Shepherds Lane close to dinner time and they prepared to part company. Lewis tossed his duffle bag by the front door and tapped the living room window where the dogs were doing somersaults at his return. After their long talk, Todd appeared determined to find some other avenue for investment that was less risky than emu eggs.

Todd leaned from the driver's window with a smile.

'You might get something in the mail from me soon.'

'What's that?' Lewis strolled back to the car, glad to see Todd's faith in his future restored.

'A wedding invitation.'

'You're going to propose to your girl?'

'Saturday. I'm taking Katie to that swanky restaurant

down the coast. The Blue Lagoon Winery. Do you think she'll have me?'

Katie Taylor, the young lady in question, was the only daughter of one of the district's farming families. Her father had a thousand acres in sheep and cattle, and he was known to not suffer fools lightly.

'Absolutely. Aren't you the best catch in Limetree?' Todd taught maths and science at the local high school and lived alone at the teachers' residence. His dress sense was somewhat wanting. 'Come to us an hour before you get Katie. Alice and I will make sure you look your best.'

'Okay. That would be great.'

'Get a haircut, Todd. And make sure you buy a new shirt and tie.'

Todd stroked his hair where it touched his collar. 'Gosh. Really?'

'You want this moment to be memorable. Have you got a ring?'

'Yep. I've got that sorted.' Todd started to back down the driveway. 'Thanks for your advice today,' he shouted. 'See you on Saturday.'

A wedding invitation. I suppose that means I'll have to bring a partner. There were times when being himself was complicated. Half the town would be expecting Louise to attend a social event like this. The other half would be expecting Lewis.

     Kayleen M. Hazlehurst

The appointment with Alice and Louise was for five o'clock, and Todd arrived on time in a nicely polished car. Within half an hour his wrinkled trousers, snatched away by Alice, had been given a good iron. Louise saw his new silk tie needed adjusting. Silk ties could be slippery. They were devils to knot and to ensure the wide end was long enough. His collar was straightened and his hair given an extra comb to subdue the ducktail. (He'd forgotten to get a haircut.)

The young suitor was duly dispatched with a tiny rose bud in his lapel and carrying a bunch of roses from Louise's garden, wrapped in coloured cellophane paper and tied with a ribbon. Alice and Louise stood on the doorstep to wave him away like anxious parents.

Alice chuckled. 'If the poor thing wasn't nervous before he came, he certainly is now.'

'Let's hope Katie is gracious and kind.'

'Yes. There's nothing like a sensible girl to help a man get on his feet.'

Louise looked at Alice and saw she was teary, remembering perhaps her own husband's proposal all those years ago. The situation was reminiscent of an Ella Fitzgerald song the choir had been practising. Everyone's favourite.

'*Someday he'll come along,*' Louise crooned in an alto voice, putting an arm around Alice's shoulder. '*The man I love …*'

Alice smiled and punched Louise in the arm. 'Stop it, you.'

She took an exaggerated breath. '*And, he'll be big and strong …*' She raised her eyebrows at Alice a couple of times.

'*The man I love …*' Alice joined in.

'*And when he comes my way, I'll do my best to make him stay,*' they sang in unison as they sauntered back into the house.

⚜

The engagement between Todd Finch and Katie Taylor was announced in the *Limetree Gazette*. Catering for a large wedding would take some planning, and the café would probably be asked to provide a few cakes. The wedding breakfast was to be served at the Taylor homestead. Three hundred guests were not unusual for families so deeply rooted in farming districts.

Lewis wondered what he should do. The safest thing was to invite his wife as his wedding partner. He understood why she had wanted the separation. Jessica was hurt when he ran away to Limetree to experiment with his alter ego.

     Kayleen M. Hazlehurst

He hoped she had forgiven him. They had stayed friends in the four years they'd been apart, telephoning each other occasionally. *I'll give her a call, just in case.*

Jessica Hammond responded with warmth to his call.

'A country wedding would be fabulous,' she said. 'I'd like to get out of the city. I've been unemployed for three months.'

This was news to Lewis. The last he'd heard she had a job at an accountant's office.

'You're not working?'

'Between jobs.' Jessica spoke in an upbeat tone, clearly trying to hide how miserable she was. When he probed, she admitted she'd been seeing her boss. The relationship had fallen over when she discovered the man was married.

'Are you okay?' he asked.

'Of course. I'd love to see your café, Lewis. I hear it's quite the thing. There was an article …'

'I'll introduce you to the girls.'

Alice seemed excited to meet 'the wife', she hadn't even known there was one. Lewis never spoke about his private life. 'My, you're a cagey one.'

Todd's wedding was set for late summer, 12 February 1994. Jessica was to drive up from Auckland the day before and stay the weekend in Lewis' spare bedroom.

⟞⟝⟞⟝

Close to Christmas Lewis received another call from Todd. William Taylor, the future father-in-law, was planning to give Katie and Todd a few acres as a wedding present.

'Alpacas! Alpacas!' Todd cried down the phone.

'What?'

'Alpacas have been around for a while. What do you think of them?'

'Seem nice enough animals.'

In 1986 there had been several importations of exotic farm animals. Of the ostrich, emu, llama and water buffalo brigade, camelids were shaping up as the most popular. Of these, alpacas were the hot favourites.

Normally gentle beasts, halfway in size between a sheep and a cow, alpacas could be troublesome at shearing time—stamping and spitting with surprising range and accuracy. This meant they had to be harnessed when they were being shorn. Apart from shearing, and the need to check their toenails and teeth regularly, they were said to be easier to care for than sheep.

Todd explained why he thought alpacas might be just right for him and his new bride. They were capable

     Kayleen M. Hazlehurst

breeders, good guardians of other farm creatures, including lambs and hens, while producing three to five kilograms of silky wool in colours ranging from cream to brown. Virtually all the wool was sold domestically to a flourishing market of spinners and weavers. Farmers' wives interested in handicraft were often keen to convert alpaca wool into yarn suitable for knitwear, shawls and throw rugs. These cottage industries could enhance the income of hobby farmers.

'The farm work will have to be done on top of your teaching,' Lewis cautioned.

'I know, but at least the livestock will be ours. No-one pulling the wool over our eyes like the emu business.' Todd laughed loudest at his own jokes.

'Is Katie on board with this? It will mean extra work for her as well, and someone has to do the books.'

'It was Katie who suggested alpacas. We can start slow and build up our stock over time. Our goal is to breed the animals for their wool with no middle man. Like big sheep, really.'

'Knobbly-kneed sheep who spit.'

Todd roared. 'Exactly.'

'What does Mr Taylor think?'

'He said it was a good project for me to cut my teeth on. Promised to let me know if he thought I was going off the rails.'

'With all that help I'm sure you'll be in a safe position. Keep your investments modest and let them grow naturally.'

'Thanks Lewis. That's what I hoped you'd say.'

'On a more important note, are you looking forward to the wedding?'

'Can't come soon enough. This is the most exciting time of my life.'

'Good man. We'll all be there on your special day.'

'Hey, who will be coming with you? Did you find yourself a partner?'

'Ah-ha. You'll have to wait and see.'

'Going to keep the whole town guessing, eh?'

'You bet.'

'Funny you should say that. Down at the pub I heard they are taking bets on who you would come as.'

⊰⊱

In the end Jessica chose for him. She brought up his tuxedo and best suit, neither of which he had needed since he left Auckland. On the Friday night she unzipped the plastic suit bag and ran her hand over the dark clothing. The release of a telling fragrance indicated she'd had them both dry-cleaned.

'You used to look splendid in these,' she said. 'Is it

black tie or smart suit?'

'The suit will be fine. Don't want to outshine the groom.'

Lewis remembered how beautiful Jessica had looked in her blue velvet evening gown. They'd made quite a pair at their last event, just before everything fell apart.

The old lady was standing behind them smiling. 'You'll look like James Bond in that outfit,' Alice said. 'No-one will recognise you.'

Jessica regarded Lewis with her hazel eyes. 'Is that what you want, Lewis? No-one to recognise you?' She blushed. 'I'm sorry, I shouldn't have brought these back to you.'

'No, it was an excellent idea, Jess. The navy suit will be perfect. Slightly understated, while still respectful towards the hosts.'

Alice lifted her hands in delight. 'We shall all dress up for the occasion. What about you, Jessica? Show us what you are wearing. Lewis and I love to give fashion tips.'

'Yes. You can poke through my jewellery if you like.'

Alice laughed. 'Oh, Lewis. You are a hoot. Don't take any notice of him. I'm sure you have much better jewellery.'

His wife's face flushed again. 'I certainly hope so. Maybe you should wear my jewellery and I should wear your suit.'

'Touché.' Lewis touched her elbow. 'Don't be anxious, Jess. It's great you're here. We'll have fun at the wedding. I promise.'

Jessie wiped her eyes with the back of her hand. 'How can I not be anxious? I've lost my marriage and my job. Now what do I have?'

Lewis stood locked in silence. She was right, he had abandoned her. After years of misgivings he still didn't know whether he'd sorted himself out.

Alice put her arm around the back of the younger woman. 'You have a friend in Lewis, that's what you have. You have here a very dear friend.'

'I'm going to cry if you keep being so damn kind.'

Bentley approached and put his head under her hand.

'Meet Doctor Dog,' Lewis said. 'He thinks he's a psychologist.'

'I can believe it.'

They all laughed.

'Now, my girl,' Alice guided Jessica to a comfortable chair. 'You sit down while I make us all a nice cup of tea.'

Jessica flopped down on the seat and Bentley placed his head on her knee. 'Let me know if Doctor Dog sires any puppies. I'd like to have one.'

Lewis smiled and touched the dog's head. 'You'll be the first to know.'

 Kayleen M. Hazlehurst

SEVEN

A Country Wedding

1994

ALICE WOKE TO the sound of weeping. She knocked on the guest room door and quietly stepped inside.

'Are you all right, dear?' Their visitor was curled among a jumbled heap of bedding as if she'd been fighting with the sheets all night. 'Whatever is the matter?'

Jessica sucked in a breath between her sobs. 'I have to talk to Lewis.'

'All right,' Alice said cautiously. 'Can it wait until breakfast?'

'No. It's important.'

'Oh well, we had to get up early, anyway.'

'You must have so much to do before the wedding.'

'A few sandwiches for the children, that's all. We baked the cakes yesterday.'

'Aren't you providing the lunch?'

'No, thank goodness. An Auckland company is doing the catering.'

Jessica ran her fingers through her unruly mop of brown hair. 'I must look a fright.'

Alice hooked her arm around the younger woman's shoulders and drew her into a hug. 'Wash your face while I put on the kettle. You can borrow that dressing gown in the cupboard.'

'Will you wake Lewis?'

'I'll do it right away. We can gather in the kitchen.'

Alice prepared their English Breakfast in front of the kitchen window. There was no hint of daylight or sounds of early traffic, and the birds had barely stirred. Woken animals were milling underfoot. She had served out their biscuits, aware of their quirks and obsessions, and called each pet to their bowl.

Lewis stumbled into the doorway. 'What's up?' he asked, tightening the cord of his waistband. He appeared somewhat comical in his men's striped pyjamas, pink dressing gown and fluffy slippers.

Jessica took one look at him and howled.

Stunned, Lewis opened his mouth then closed it again.

'There, there,' Alice said firmly. 'Tears will do no good at all. Come now, let's sit at the table.' She set down

 Kayleen M. Hazlehurst

three strong mugs of tea and turned to Lewis. 'Jessica has something important to tell you.'

Lewis took hold of Jessica's trembling hand. 'What is it, Jess? Why you are so distraught?'

'That's right.' Alice said. 'Talk to us, dear. You'll feel so much better.'

'I'm pregnant!' Jessica blurted out. 'I discovered it just before I left Auckland.'

Alice gave a gentle sway of her head. 'Well then, that isn't so terrible. What do you think, Lewis?'

He regarded the woman, who had once been his wife, not sure how he felt about this revelation. 'You're only thirty-six. What does the doctor say?'

'He says … He says I'm fit and healthy, but—'

'Hang on. Weren't we an infertile couple during our marriage? That's why we never—'

Jessica plucked at the edge of the tablecloth. 'This is Steven's baby.'

Lewis frowned. 'Your accountant friend.'

'My so-called friend who admits he has a wife after months of breathing hot and cold.'

'I'm so sorry, Jess. That was a rotten trick to play on you.'

'Steven will never acknowledge this child.'

Alice fell silent for a long moment. 'Could this be a

blessing?' she said at last. 'I've seen many last-chance babies come out of adversity. Yet these children grew up to be a great comfort to the mothers who lost husbands and sweethearts during the war.'

'Alice is right. It sometimes helps to put things in perspective.'

'But I'm alone,' Jessica wailed. 'And I don't know a thing about babies!'

'Don't be silly, dear. You have friends. You have us. This child will be loved.'

Lewis remained calm while Jessica blew her nose on a tissue. He couldn't believe he was actually jealous of the sod. 'A baby, Jess. How exciting. I always knew you'd make a wonderful mum.'

According to Alice, the best way to deal with an upset was through 'good honest work'. She turned to Jessica. 'We'd welcome an extra pair of hands this morning. Will you join us?'

'You mean at the café?'

'Just for a couple of hours.'

'I'd love to. Will Gail and Jenny be there?'

'We're closed for the weekend, but you'll meet the girls at the wedding.'

⤙⤙⤙⟢

 Kayleen M. Hazlehurst

After breakfast they took two cars to work. Lewis looked at the wall clock as soon as they arrived. Six o'clock. 'We have three hours to get everything done.'

Alice tied on an apron and started to lay down slices of Tip Top bread on the counter.

'When does the service begin?' Jessica asked Lewis.

He studied the clock again. 'Eleven o'clock. If we want a seat at the church we'll have to leave the house early.'

'We'll be ready,' Alice assured him. 'Jessie, can you take over this buttering?' They exchanged places and Alice took out two dozen eggs from the fridge. She stopped to put one hand on her hip. 'Who will take our food to the organisers?'

Lewis extracted a large saucepan from the bottom shelf, added hot water from the electric jug and placed it on the stove. 'I'll do the deliveries. That will give you ladies time to have the first showers. It will be quite a party. Wonder what they'll feed us.'

Alice gave a birdlike chortle as she lowered eggs, two at a time, into the water. 'I'll eat anything as long as it's not cakes and sandwiches.'

Jessica started furiously buttering. 'Shall I do some slices with sprinkles?'

'Good idea,' Lewis said. 'Children love sprinkles on ice cream.'

'Oh, what about ice cream?'

'The caterers should bring a selection of tubs.'

After four minutes Lewis lifted an egg with a tablespoon to watch it dry in the steam. 'Cooked. Want me to shell and mash these?'

Alice slid the eggs into a bowl of cold water. 'We'd better all do the shelling or we'll never get away.'

Jessica took her share of eggs on a tea towel. 'You two work so well together.'

Alice laughed. 'We've got it down pat.'

'I'm so curious about Limetree. I bet you'll know everyone at the wedding, Alice.'

'The locals are on the bride's side, but the groom's people are from the city. I'll not know many of them.'

'You're lucky. I won't know a soul ... Do you have any mayonnaise and parsley?'

Alice passed Jessica a large jar of mayonnaise. 'It won't take you long to make new friends ... There's a parsley plant in a pot by the back door ... Can someone please find me four large plates for these sandwiches?'

❦

Louise woke around three to the faint trill of an early-rising quail. The small brown-and-white birds seldom lived near the towns, but clutches of ten or more chicks could be seen scampering after their vigilant

 Kayleen M. Hazlehurst

parents in the fields and grasslands where the wild pheasants roamed.

She lay in the dark, sensing she was in a strange bed but was not alone. Alice and Jessie were sleeping in rooms further down the hall, but the snoring hump in the corner had a distinct Bentley tone. In quieter moments it was easy to slip in and out of her feminine persona. She put a hand on her sore head. Yesterday was Todd and Katie's wedding. A grand event, attended by half the local district and a crowd of their city friends. *All that flowing wine and champagne.*

After the church ceremony the guests had driven ten kilometres north to the bride's home. On the front lawn of a dignified country villa a marquee had been set up to shade several rows of white-clothed tables and canvas chairs to cater for the wedding of the Taylors' only child.

From a long counter, staff in white aprons served food from tureens and steel service pans. Louise was especially interested that the spread bore a 'country fare' theme. A blackboard menu poised on top of straw bales listed a choice of mushroom and basil pasta, smoked fish pie, pork cutlets, lamb casserole, chicken curry, ham on the bone, or roast beef sliced up with lashings of gravy. Half a side of beef was roasting on a spit in the forecourt.

At the side, diners could help themselves to a buffet

of salads and hot vegetables, as well as an assortment of desserts. The blend of aromas was enough to set off anyone's taste buds.

After speeches, squares of a four-tier wedding cake were handed around the tables. The crooning guitarist and his pretty singer on the small podium were almost drowned out by the chatter, but nobody seemed to mind. Faces gleamed and Louise assumed that all the workers were being well compensated. Most of the serving staff were probably relatives.

During the reception Lewis' women friends had commented on the 'dashing figure' he cut in his suit, and 'how lovely' his partner looked in her cream lace dress and linen jacket. With a beer in his hand fellows, normally uncomfortable around Louise, shared jokes with Lewis or commiserated on how poorly the Black Caps had performed in this summer's cricket tour of Australia. How Shane Warne was a freak of nature, and how Martin Crowe had been sorely missed after his knee injury. It was all very civil and Lewis knew exactly how to play the roles expected of him.

By late afternoon guests had departed for their homes and hotels, where celebrations may have continued into the night.

Alice, who believed it was hazardous to share an

 Kayleen M. Hazlehurst

unlit highway with even one inebriated driver, had suggested the day before that Lewis and Jessica bring their toothbrushes and a change of clothes so they could stay Saturday night at her farmhouse.

'I need to check up on a few things, anyway.'

'We'd love to visit your place, wouldn't we Jess?'

'Absolutely. I'll pack a little case.'

If half the town went to bed drunk as lords on Saturday night no-one would have been surprised, although Alice appeared to be looking for an excuse to show off her property to Jessica. An enticement, perhaps, to encourage her to move to Limetree.

The prospect of a baby joining their incongruous and cobbled together family had set off maternal instincts in the old girl. Within hours of the pregnancy announcement, even before Lewis and Jessica had found time to resolve their mutually disastrous lives, Alice had become as clucky as a mother quail.

Lewis switched on the bedside lamp and pulled on his jeans and jumper. He walked to the bathroom with the roused dog at his heels. When he came out Bentley wagged his tail and gave a polite whimper, indicating he too needed to relieve himself.

'Come on, boy.' He reached for the light switch at the top of the staircase. 'Try not to be noisy.'

They padded down the staircase on the thickly woven Axminster. This red and gold carpeting, soft under the soles of bare feet, had become popular after the war in households that could afford the luxury. When they entered the backyard, they stopped to breathe in the warm February air—sweetened by the smells of late summer pastures, the vigorous haymaking on surrounding farms, and the moist mists rising up from creeks and frog ponds.

Bentley took a moment to sniff among the flowerbeds, perhaps recalling the garden from the day he'd helped find Alice after she went missing.

'Good boy. You know this place, eh?' A shiver passed through Lewis. 'Come on, we'd better go back inside. There's time for a little more kip.'

Bentley turned his nose to the dark sky and stood motionless. Far away another dog was barking. Lewis paused to listen. Had the neighbouring canine spotted a rabbit, or was he hopeful of an early breakfast before the milking?

'It's nothing.'

Bentley disagreed. He sat on his tail and answered with a low, chilling moan.

'Quiet. You'll wake the ladies. Let's go.'

     Kayleen M. Hazlehurst

Lewis clicked off the light switch at the top of the staircase and immediately sensed something was wrong. At the end of the hallway the pitched window facing north glowed. He strode into the sewing room and stretched up to look out the attic window. On the edge of the forest his eye was drawn to a streak of orange.

At first it was a thin line, then it flared and spread higher and wider ... One football field ... two football fields ... three football fields.

'My God!'

Wildfire was raging over the dry landscape at an appalling speed.

He raced down the hall to waken the women, not sure which was Jessica's room.

'Wake up!' he shouted. 'Alice ... Jessie ... Wake up!'

He thumped on the walls and doors, almost tripping over his own feet. Behind him Bentley was barking, electrified by his master's urgency. Jessica came out, her eyes wide.

'What is it, Lewis? You're scaring me.'

'There's fire in the foothills. It's got into the scrub and dry grass. We're right in its path.' He turned when he felt a cool hand on his arm.

Alice had silently joined them. She was standing beside him in a multicoloured dressing gown with the stillness of age and experience. 'There's only us and the dog. I have no other animals here. How bad is it?'

He gestured towards the sewing room. 'See for yourself.'

Jessica was rushing down the hall turning on lights. She grabbed the sewing chair and climbed up to look out the top window.

'Ah-h-h! … Oh, Alice, you have to see this.'

Jessica got down and helped Alice onto the chair.

'Call the Fire Service, Lewis. I'll ring Katie's parents. The Taylor property backs onto the grassland.'

Jessica pawed at her hair. 'We have to get out of here!'

Lewis agreed. 'Okay. You've got time to put on your clothes and gather your things. I'll get Bentley into the truck. Be quick, Jess.'

'I can take my car,' said Alice. 'I know which farm-houses to rouse. Can you and Jessie warn the village?'

'Don't take too long, Alice. Two more phone calls, then you must leave. Promise me. That fire is travelling fast.'

'I promise.'

After dialling emergency services, Lewis bundled Bentley and Jessica into his truck. The sky was reddening and a wind had whipped up, driving the flames forward.

Alice only had a house and some outbuildings to worry about, nothing she would put before people or

    Kayleen M. Hazlehurst

animals. Scattered around her were many friends. Farming families with precious stock. The old lady could be entrusted with the task of warning them.

Lewis considered how the farmers might deal with this. Country people wouldn't ask for help unless they first helped themselves. Most would stay to protect their properties or they would join the firefighters in stopping the spread.

Limetree was a different matter.

If wildfire got into the village it would jump from house to house, fuelled by the wooden structures. Worse still, it was early Sunday morning.

Most of the residents would be sleeping.

EIGHT

The Small Miracle of Limetree

THE ROAD WAS almost empty as Lewis, Jessica and Bentley hurtled down the highway, blasting their horn as they passed houses. They would have to leave the rest up to the telephone trees of caring people.

Their first stop was at the Limetree police station. A new recruit was on night duty. Lewis rattled the door and the officer stared at him through the glass. Judging by his scowl he was expecting a quiet shift.

'There's a fire coming!' Lewis shouted. 'We need to raise the alarm. Can you alert Sergeant Winfield?'

The door was reluctantly opened. 'This is a joke, right?'

'Not unless you want your tail singed. Tell the sergeant Lewis Hammond called it in.'

'The Sarg' won't be happy. It's four in the morning.'

'Just do it, son! We'll start waking everyone but it'll be faster if the police helped. The fire brigade should be tearing through here any minute.'

Larger towns nearby had fire engines and two fire crews had been promised within forty-five minutes. Lewis expected teams of volunteers to follow. The farmers would set up their own crews to beat the earth. They caught the distant sound of a siren and Lewis raised his eyebrows at the young copper.

The officer became suddenly animated. 'I'll call Sergeant Winfield. I'm Andy Lowden, by the way. What else can I do?'

'Call as many people as you can. Tell them a huge blaze is barrelling down on the town.'

'Bloody, hell!'

Lewis headed back to the truck with Constable Lowden pursuing him down the path.

'This is Andy,' Lewis told Jessica. 'Andy … Jessica.'

'Gidday, Jessica.'

'Hello,' she replied. 'Lewis, we'd better get going.'

'What's the plan? Give me something to tell the sergeant.'

'We'll start with the houses then move on to the shops. Some people live on those premises.'

'Like that Indian family at the corner store?'

'Yes. The Bashis occupy the back of the store and the Coopers live above the bakery.'

'The police could do the commercial end of town. Make sure everyone's out of those buildings.'

'That would be good, Andy. Perhaps you could start by phoning.'

'I'll go through the phone directory while I'm waiting for the sergeant.'

Jessica smiled at Lewis. 'You see. Lots of people will help us.'

The policeman looked forlorn. 'There are towns that have sirens to announce public emergencies ...'

'Yeah. Pity we don't. All we can do is go around blasting our horns and banging on doors.'

Bentley stuck his head out the window to examine Lewis' companion.

'Oh, and can we leave Bentley with you?'

'Who?'

'Sergeant Winfield's search and rescue dog.' Lewis coaxed Bentley onto the pavement and handed over the lead. 'He'll be safer at the police station. Put him in a cell with a bowl of water.'

'Hey, we could be HQ. Meet us back at the station so we can plan strategies.'

Lewis shook his head. 'No time, Andy. Let's make the park the assembly point. We'll tell people to go there so the police can tick off their names. Make sure no-one is lost ... Sorry, have to go.'

'The park ... Righto.'

Lewis put the truck into gear and started to move.

'Good luck!' Andy shouted as they tore off down Main Street.

They fell silent for a moment, feeling Bentley's absence in the truck.

'Should we telephone your friends from the house?' Jessica asked.

'It's probably better to make one hell of a noise. Get people out of bed without having to give long explanations. Have you got a woollen jumper for your arms in case of flying sparks, and a scarf to cover your nose.'

'For the smoke?'

'If it comes to it.' They swung into the first side street. 'Here we go.'

'Hope Alice is okay.' Jessica's last words were drowned out as Lewis drove the heel of his hand into the horn.

House lights were coming on. Lewis slammed on his brakes and they leapt from the vehicle to take one side of the street each.

'FIRE! FIRE! WE HAVE TO EVACUATE!' they

     Kayleen M. Hazlehurst

yelled as they dashed from house to house. 'YOU MUST GET OUT!'

A muscular, red-faced man was the first to confront Lewis. It was the local garbage collector preparing for an early start.

'What the …?'

'Kevin. Thank goodness. Fire has got into the scrub north of here and it's coming towards the town. The whole village is in danger.'

Kevin sniffed the wind and noted the red glow in the sky. 'Have the firies been called?'

'Already on the road. Can you wake your neighbours? Watch out for summer visitors, tents and caravans. The park is the assembly point. People need to identify themselves to the police before they leave town. We have to make sure everyone's been told.'

'Gotcha,' Kevin said, his face shining with conviction. 'Thanks, mate. You go on. I'll deal with this street.'

News travelled fast. The willingness of the locals to join in the alert allowed Lewis and Jessica to keep moving. Their knuckles were bruised from thumping on doors. Soon the town was abuzz with shouting adults, barking dogs, and children in blankets being bundled into cars. Holidaymakers were already fleeing and clogging up the roads.

Lewis paused to speak with Jessica. 'We'd better go home to rescue Alice's pets.'

'Hope they haven't run away.'

'Gail was feeding them but they could be frightened.'

'She might have already picked them up.'

'It's possible. But I'd like to make sure the girls have been warned.'

'Of course, we must call them.'

'As long as the lines aren't down. If the fire reaches the town we could lose power … the school … the church …'

'The fire brigade should be able to …'

'I don't know.'

'Oh, Lewis … Bentley? … What about the police station?'

'Not if Sergeant Winfield has anything to do with it. Ronald loves that station.'

They arrived at Shepherds Lane to see people on the move. Lewis parked in front of his garage and stepped onto the concrete driveway. He checked the sky. Since he'd been watching he had seen growing evidence of the approaching fire. A sheaf of grey cast the whole town into a strange kind of dawn. Further away, a column of acrid smoke was billowing down from the north-west.

     Kayleen M. Hazlehurst

This wasn't just smouldering grassland, where a grader had been used to create a firebreak. Light was reflecting off the clouds in the way flames might illuminate the sky. The fire had reached the edge of Limetree and the village had started to burn.

'We'll grab a few things. Get the animals. Make sure no-one on the street has been forgotten.'

Sadie and Cleo could not be found. Lewis and Jessica assured each other that they'd already been collected. It was impossible to check because the phones no longer worked.

'Alice would have called Jenny and Gail after we left the farmhouse,' Jessica said.

'You're probably right. She'd be worried about her pets.'

They looked around the backyard and found the orphaned magpie shivering under a large leaf of silver beet.

Lewis offered his hand. 'Here, little one. You'd better come with us. Flying might be difficult in this air.'

'I'll grab the shoe box off the back table.'

'Put some fresh water in the jar lid, Jess.'

'Okay. And I'll get us a couple of water bottles.'

He could feel the bird's heart beating hard against the flesh of his palm. When they weren't closed, the whites of the magpie's eyes almost dominated the pupils. The noise and smoke, and the loss of his friends, had left the creature traumatised.

'Oh, Maggie, I'm so sorry. Hey Jess, find some mince for the bird in the freezer. I don't think he's eaten for a couple of days.'

When they exited the house with their few belongings—the dog beds, some pet biscuits, a loaf of bread, tins of tuna and baked beans, the bird in the shoebox with holes punched into the lid—they were shocked to see how much the wind had fanned the blaze.

Two kilometres away, maybe closer, the dry crowns of trees were igniting like Olympic torches, showering the sky with sparks. Corrugated iron was flying off garage roofs. They could hear the snarl of the beast, the crash of collapsing buildings, the occasional *boom* of a gas cylinder or exploding car. Australians he'd once talked to had told him the darkness and noise of an inferno were the most terrible things. They were.

Lewis was sure the fire had shifted between them and the park. Thickening smoke was clawing at their throats and they felt skin-tightening heat on their faces. It was too late to jump into the truck and take off. He didn't want the vehicle becoming another fireball. His only hope was that everyone had got away.

 Kayleen M. Hazlehurst

He took Jessica's hand in his. 'We can't risk driving into the path of the flames, Jess. We've a better chance if we dampen our surroundings and stay where we are. I've got two hoses at the front. I'll wet down the building if you'll do the truck and the lawn. If we put out spot fires we might save the street.'

They covered their mouths and noses with cotton towels and wound the hoses around their wrists for grip, turning them on each other until they were soaked to the skin. Then they focused the water in two directions—the front of the section towards the street, and the roof and siding of the house.

'Oh, Lewis. Are we completely alone?'

'We'll know once this smoke clears.'

There they were, back-to-back, protecting each other against the elements. Nature had turned against them and all they could do now was guard each other and their ridiculous little lives. Yet he was glad she was standing beside him.

'I love you Lou,' she whispered.

He glanced around at her. 'That's the first time you've called me Lou.'

'Maybe it's my way of acknowledging who you are. A combination of your names,' she said. 'Alice accepts you and I'm ashamed I never did. I'll do better if you help me to understand.'

'I could have played things differently,' he answered. 'I'm sorry for being so self-obsessed.' He gave a short chuckle. 'We have a lot in common, you and me. If we get out of this mess would you give us another go, Jess?'

She shrieked. 'God, you pick your moments!'

It would have been funny, were they not coughing and wiping their eyes as much as they were laughing at the lunacy of it all.

Through the haze they began to see slowly moving shapes … Vehicles pulling up … A fire truck preceded by three or four figures in high-visibility suits.

At the front of the rescuers was a large black dog pulling with all his might on a lead.

'Bentley!' Jessica cried.

Lewis laughed. 'Well, if it isn't Sergeant Winfield!'

'Trying to make yourselves bloody heroes?' Winfield growled.

'No. Just giving you the chance to show off.'

'I'll thank you not to wake me so early on a Sunday morning.'

'Sorry, Sergeant ... *Awarff!*' That was all Lewis had time to say before he was hit full in the chest by an exuberant canine.

'Good boy,' said Jessica, patting Bentley's head as he stood over the flattened Lewis to lick his face.

 Kayleen M. Hazlehurst

'Aren't you just the best search and rescue dog in the whole world!'

Winfield looked pleased and the fire crew gave Lewis the thumbs up.

'Come on you two,' the sergeant said. 'Get in your truck and follow our police car. Let these boys to do their job with the fire truck.'

'Is it safe to leave?'

'We'll show you the way.'

Experiencing the emergency first-hand had given Lewis a lot to think about. Wildfires had been increasing in frequency and intensity throughout the country, and he wondered whether this latest catastrophe was caused by a lightning strike, a careless hunter in the forest, or some idiot tossing out a cigarette from his car.

He was filled with admiration for the firefighters. They had battled the grassfire with the help of the farmers, plunged on to protect the village, and put themselves unflinchingly between the flames and people's homes.

In the forthcoming weeks the *Limetree Gazette* provided many colourful eyewitness accounts of that day in February 1994. Later, the editor would reflect on the event:

The small miracle of Limetree was that nobody was hurt in the fire. Our farmers fought tooth and nail to slow down the blaze. No farmhouses or stock were lost. The destruction was limited to three haystacks, four rural outbuildings, one warehouse, half-a-dozen scorched shops, twenty-five damaged houses, and a number of burnt-out vehicles. Because people pulled together our school and church were saved.

The effects of any fire are heart breaking, and it was a sad community that returned to the task of cleaning up. But if a farming district is anything, it is resilient. The first thing the council has promised us is the installation of a public alert siren.

These human stories will be woven into our history. They will become part of the folk memory of our region. There was pride in the heroic service of our firefighters, in the swift action of our police to organise the evacuation, and in the courageous sniffer dogs who went out with police in search of people unaccounted for.

The Fire Service was quoted as saying that if the warning had come thirty minutes later, it would have been a far greater tragedy. This was attributed to residents rousing each other

     Kayleen M. Hazlehurst

and making their escape. There was mention of two people, a man and a woman, going around thumping on doors but no-one was certain who they were.

On behalf of the town, the *Limetree Gazette* thanks you all.

Postscript

2011

A MAN IN his early sixties spoke in gentle tones to Titan, his tan Labrador, as they worked over broken rock and debris in a pattern of sweeps.

The Christchurch earthquake struck at 12.51 pm on Tuesday, 22 February 2011, and continued to release energy from its city epicentre in outward waves of aftershocks. Teams of police, firefighters, paramedics and search and rescue personnel with their precious equipment and dogs arrived just hours after the quake hit.

An amalgamated response centre was set up in the modern, quake-resistant Christchurch Art Gallery with the event declared as a civil defence emergency. Security cordons were placed around parts of the central city that had suffered the worst effects from the quake. The New Zealand Fire Service co-ordinated the Urban Search and Rescue teams that were coming quickly from all corners of New Zealand, Australia, and more distant corners of the globe.

Buried beneath this pile of rubble were survivors and it was their job to find them.

The Hammonds were among the first of the North Island responders. After stuffing their backpacks with a change of clothes and toiletries and driving their best dogs in transport cages to the Whenuapai Airport, they took the special emergency flight to Christchurch. They were welcomed onto the scene by a small group of exhausted local rescuers who had already been working for thirty-six hours. The number of civilian deaths was yet unknown, but the devastation was obvious.

The central city and eastern suburbs had suffered intense damage from collapsed buildings and liquefaction. Liquefaction—a word for 'bloody awful stuff' few people had heard of before that day—was politely described as 'silt'. Tonnes and tonnes of water and sand disgorged from the earth and turned hard ground into deep sucking mud. It cracked roads and bridges, crushed buses and cars, and destabilised the foundations of every brick home, concrete workplace, and solid stone church in its wake. This was the horror that met the eyes of emergency workers as they entered the *Red Zone* at the restricted heart of the city.

 Kayleen M. Hazlehurst

The wildfire back in 1994 had been cathartic for many Limetree residents. For Lewis, it had inspired a lifelong interest in the emergency services.

Following the birth of Samuel, he and Jessica had moved to the Blakely farm on Alice's invitation. The old lady's generosity to the couple, along with a realisation that they still loved each other, turned out to be all the pith and fibre they needed to rebuild their fragmented lives.

Louise continued to work part-time at the café with the help of the girls. Lewis and Jessica were installed as managers on a property that would have otherwise gone under the real estate hammer. Little Samuel was given a stable home life, and Alice returned to her old nest as honorary Grandma and baker of cookies and cakes.

Naturally, all their pets came with them. Sadie, Cleo, Maggie and Bentley. Labradors were known to be smart, brave and empathetic. Starting with the good genetic material of Bentley, a breeding and certification programme for search and rescue dogs grew into a family vocation. Over the next seventeen years many of their dogs became star pupils in this specialised area of training. Like Bentley, they found their niche in life.

Lewis smiled over at the young man not far from him, who was working with their other dog, Gypsy, on a different pile of rubble that had once been an office block. The eagerness of Titan and Gypsy's movements expressed an intelligence and heightened sense of urgency. The shared understanding between the search dogs and their handlers was a clear testament to their years of training and experience.

'We'll move to the back of the building after we've finished here,' Lewis called out. 'I'm hoping we'll find a shaft or a passageway near a door.'

For Samuel, who had grown up with several generations of clever canines, search and rescue was his passion. He wouldn't hear of being left behind when the call to duty came. The sixteen-year-old was as skilled as any adult dog-handler, and Lewis loved working with him. Jessica took turns on the short-wave radio, helping with communications between the field crews and paramedics, and eighty-year-old Alice was left at home to look after things on the farm.

Titan yelped, then staring down he started to bark. It was that loud, wide-mouthed bark that he only used when he'd caught the scent of a live human being underground.

'Good, boy, Titan. Good boy.'

Sam rushed over with Gypsy and the two dogs scouted an area of about five square metres. Now they were both yelping and barking, eyes fixed to the ground.

 Kayleen M. Hazlehurst

'They've found something, Dad!'

'I think you're right, Sammy. Could be several of them down there.'

Five survivors were pulled from that spot. Lewis and Samuel left them to the rescuers and moved on with their dogs in search of more trapped souls.

Kayleen Hazlehurst was born in Warkworth, North Auckland, and began to write stories and poetry as a child growing up on a farm beside the Mahurangi River. Her research and advocacy as an anthropologist took her to remote communities in  the Canadian Arctic, United States, Australia and New Zealand. She later retrained as a medical herbalist and naturopath.

Kayleen's work reflects an empathy with nature and a passionate interest in social issues. Her two recent novels are family sagas of love and war. *A Caramel Sky* is about the air defence and intelligence missions of the Royal New Zealand Air Force, set in the Pacific Islands and the Home Front during the Pacific War. *Who Disturbs the Kūkupa?* is a story of courage and survival during the ANZAC campaigns in Greece, Crete and Italy, particularly those of the 28th Māori Battalion.

She now divides her time between New Zealand and Australia, where she has families.